Maplebrook Bridge

Maplebrook Bridge

❋ *Snowfall Wishes* ❋

JENNIFER GRIFFITH

Maplebrook Bridge

ASIN: B09JHQ9HQD
ISBN: 9798751994303

This is a work of fiction. Names, characters, places, and events are creations of the author's imagination or are used fictitiously. Any resemblance to actual persons, living or dead, events, or locations, is purely coincidental.

Cover art credit: Blue Water Books

For Louise, Because of the Furniture Store

Chapter 1

Emily

"What? You're taking a lunch hour?" Brenda stopped me in the hall, grabbing my arm and almost making me drop my Tupperware. "You? Emily England, the biggest workaholic at Pokoa Financial? Knock me over with a feather." Then she broke into laughter. "Fine. At least let me come down the elevator with you—until the overlords call for me again."

"That will only take a hot second." We stepped onto the elevator at the forty-first floor of The Hancock, the most iconic building of the Boston skyline—and Pokoa never let us forget it. "They'll be breathing down your neck before you get to the seventh floor. You watch."

"But what about your neck?"

"I scheduled a meeting in my calendar." And calendared meetings—at least—were sacred. I didn't do it very often, but today I felt unsettled, as if something either really great or something really terrible was about to happen.

"You are some kind of brilliant." Brenda reached in her pocket and pulled out a baggie of crackers. "Meanwhile, we lower echelon folks are eating crackers in the elevator for our lunch break. Hey, you stuck being bridesmaid again this holiday season?"

The holidays weren't for a few months yet. "Nah, my two best friends are already married." Jayne two years ago, Mallory last year. "I'm safe from the catch-the-bouquet curse."

"Have you ever caught it, Emily? Be honest." Just then Brenda's phone did ring in the overlords' ring tone. "Hold that thought." She answered, and then hit *seven* on the elevator pad, where she got out. "Bye, now—you clairvoyant, you."

Was I clairvoyant? No, but it would explain a few of my better stock trades—and why Pokoa was smart to keep me around. I'm not conceited, but I do know my worth. There's a difference.

But Brenda's words had struck a chord. My heels tapped across the tile of the lobby and echoed the chant in my head. *I'm the last one left. My snowfall wish hasn't come true. And I was the one who told them about it. I'm the last one left. I'm the last one left.*

I actually hadn't caught the bouquet—either time.

Speed walking for exercise, I made my way to the Boston Public Garden park bench that always suited me best when I needed to think. There, next to the *Make Way for Ducklings* sculpture, I pretended to eat my lunch while, in reality, I was ruminating on my life.

Okay, I was actually surfing the internet on my usual topics: real estate, history, covered—

Shazam! Would you look at that! My eyes bugged out. It couldn't be real, but there it was in bold font.

For sale: Vermont Covered Bridge property.

A baby carrot went flying out of my mouth and landed in front of a bronze duckling as I spluttered in shock. For reals? Could a covered bridge *actually* be for sale? This had to be a hoax!

But no, a speedy search of the ownership of the remaining extant bridges in Vermont detailed that a select few were in private ownership—including this one at a small village called Maplebrook.

My teeth chattered, even though it was late summertime. I read and reread the listing. It'd been up for just two days, and an offer was pending. Aw, how horrifying. I'd almost had a chance ...

"Just a second. I'm not Emily England for nothing!" I shouted at a passing pigeon, who'd grabbed my carrot. It fluttered away, leaving a few stray feathers. I'd done enough negotiations and deals that I wouldn't miss out on something this important.

And this was important. Immensely. This—well, it was my first-snowfall wish.

In no time I'd dialed the listing agent's number and made an offer much higher than the asking price—not quite the bitter edges of my savings account, but not too far from it either.

Was it fate, or was this just me jackrabbiting after something like an impulsive lunatic? I paused for a gut-check.

No, I'd been able to hone my instincts enough to rein in impulse and only make bold moves when they made sense on a deep level.

"I'll get back to you after consulting with the property owner," the listing agent promised. "And you say you have cash, so there will be no waiting period on loan approval?"

"Cash." I was firm. And I'd get over to my bank's branch right now, if she asked me to. I could be at the property to sign paperwork as soon as tomorrow.

The agent got back to me by the time I'd eaten all my cucumber slices. "They'll take it. They had another offer on the table, but they'd had a feeling they should hold off on accepting it. You called just before the time limit. You're quite lucky."

Indeed I was! "I'll see you Friday to sign documents."

The deal would close in a mere ten days. I was ten days away from owning a covered bridge! I practically danced back to the office. It was for sure the amazing thing that my soul had sensed loomed. Thank you, gut instinct.

"Justin! You'll never believe this." I went straight for my boyfriend's corner office on our company's floor. "I bought something today, and I think you're going to love it."

"That's great, babe." Justin was staring at his computer screen. I knew to always wait for him to refocus on me, so that I could be sure he was listening. "Tell me all about it over dinner?"

"Verona's for pasta?" I guessed it could wait. All good news tasted even more delicious with a side of Italian food. "Eight o'clock."

"Let's make it nine thirty."

"Right." Probably wise, since I had work to do until at least that late. As it was, I'd probably have to come back after dinner anyhow to make up for my lost hour at lunchtime. "I'll make a reservation."

Justin worked as hard as I did, and he didn't complain when I had as many late nights at the office as he did. It might be a match made in heaven. He was smart, hardworking, handsome, and honest to a fault.

In fact, Justin just might be the one to make my teenage first-snowfall wish come true.

***

"You're going where? Podunk, Vermont?" Brenda gagged a little. "The roads all the way are too winding. I'd get carsick. Don't get carsick. Why are you leaving on a Friday anyway? You, a vacation day? Is Justin going?"

Justin still hadn't gotten back to me about the trip. I'd mentioned the covered bridge at dinner the other night—not that I'd bought it, but that he should come to Vermont with me—and he'd seemed distracted, disconnected. He'd been disconnected all summer, actually. We'd hardly had a good date since Easter.

"Justin is staying for work, but I'm going there to check out a property I bought." I told Brenda about it, describing it and showing her a photo.

"Are you completely nutso?" Brenda pushed my phone screen away. "It's a hulking mass of deterioration. *Termite* starts with a T. The phrase *terrible idea* also starts with a T. Who on earth uses their life savings to buy a bridge in the middle of nowhere? I thought you were the smartest woman in Boston. You'll topple off your pedestal if you sign that paperwork, my friend."

All that guff, however, was because Brenda didn't know about my first-snowfall wish. Back before the dawn of time, or when my friends

4

and I were sixteen, we'd all wished on the first snowfall. I'd wished to be kissed—and proposed to—on a covered bridge. Okay, by a hot, valiant hero of some kind, but that part was negotiable now that I was older.

In the past few years, Jayne and Mallory had both already received their wishes, or at least an approximation of them in a much better form than they'd dared wish as teenagers. Now it was my turn. To get her wish, Jayne had had to take a risk. So had Mallory. Of all three of us, I was the least risk-averse, so what had taken me so long?

Maybe fate didn't like my wish.

Well, I'd show fate. If I couldn't have the kiss or the proposal, I could at least have the bridge. And by Friday at noon, I'd be the happy owner of an actual covered bridge, spanning a beautiful stream in Vermont. How romantic. I could at least read romance novels on it on my vacation days.

If I started taking vacation days.

"I'll be back late Friday evening. Don't worry, I'll check in here at the office, in case there are fires to put out."

"You'd better bring your mega-size extinguisher." Brenda chuckled and sipped from her mug. "There's some bad voodoo in the air here, and I'm pretty sure they'll be asking you to don your whole fire gear for whatever it is, the minute the conflagration gets out of control, Fire Girl."

Not an unlikely scenario. "See you later. Have a good weekend." People like Brenda were familiar with the term *weekend.* Unlike me.

Weekends are for chumps. And poor people! The famous Mr. Pokoa adage said a lot about the culture at Pokoa Financial.

"You're going?" Justin passed me as I headed to the elevator. "Already?"

"It's ten p.m." Normal people were bedding down for the night.

"Yeah, but didn't you say you're going to be gone tomorrow?"

Now was my chance! He'd been too distracted when we went to Verona's the other night, and I hadn't felt like telling him all the details unless he could rejoice with me. "Yeah, I bought some property."

"Is that wise? Property prices are so high right now. Everywhere."

Um, I'd been saving up for ages—with no time to spend any money, and I'd invested well. Besides, I was poised to double my salary in the upcoming fiscal year. That is, if Justin's assessments were accurate. "Haven't you been regaling me with outrageously stratospheric projections for profits in the next few months?"

He took a call, and my chance was gone. I got on the elevator. "You're my hero," I called to him as the doors began to close.

My upstanding hero blew me a kiss.

Our next significant kiss might be under a covered bridge.

Chapter 2

Buzz

"Hiya, Buzz. Looka here. A tetch of black spot fungus." Amos popped a leaf off its stem and showed me the evidence—raised black tar dots on the top darker-green side of the maple leaf. "Just a tetch is all. Not a big deal. Won't hurt the tree none."

At least there was that. "We'll just rake up the affected leaves and trim some branches."

Other fungi, such as Verticillium wilt, would be much more detrimental—and could kill a mature tree dozens of feet high and hundreds of years old. I couldn't let anything like that happen to even a single tree of my great-grandfather's maple forest. I'd protect it at any cost—it was my last chance.

Amos took off his hat and fanned his cragged face. "Who do you think will buy the bridge yonder?" He gave a hard nod in the direction of where the covered bridge lay on the edge of Maplebrook Farm—the bridge that spanned the eponymous Maple Brook.

"Haven't heard of any sale yet."

"I hope it's not that compost-for-brains, Coolworth."

He probably meant Ivor Coolidge, the billionaire who lived a few towns over.

7

"What's the problem with Coolidge?" I'd heard Coolidge was doing the whole state a service, repairing and reinforcing any bridge he could fund. "Would having a billionaire as a neighbor be so bad?"

"Billion specks of compost for brains." Amos clearly had an opinion on the topic. "You ever heard of the word hubris? He better not touch a single splinter on my bridge or I'll—"

"Are we getting the right amount of rain for a good sap yield, do you figure?" I wasn't above interrupting one of Amos's rants.

"You'd better hope so. Don't you have that balloon payment a-coming up? I hope it's not until after the syruping."

As a matter of fact, the payment's due date fell three months before traditional sap tapping. "Last day of December."

"You gonna be able to pay it?"

If money suddenly started to grow on sugar maple trees, yeah. Absolutely.

Speaking of hubris, there were some who could argue that my decision to buy my great-grandparents' farm when Great Uncle Walter died, leaving Great Aunt Fern in a nursing home with no way to pay the bill—was hubris. Foolish pride. My dad had been raised there, but I personally hadn't been raised on a maple orchard. I hadn't lived the farm life. All I knew about the maple business I'd learned the year I spent here after my accident, plus a few summers as a kid.

Good memories. I'd even tried to build a tree house with Dad one year. It hadn't panned out, but we'd had a good time working on it a little while it lasted.

The payment loomed. Anyone who said a balloon payment was a great idea for a first-time farmer was a shyster, preying on people with pie-in-the-sky dreams like mine—the dream of being able to save Dad's childhood memories and keep them in the family.

But if I can achieve it, I'll be a family hero, too.

I mean, not like Neil. Not in the *original* meaning of the word hero, like a battle-worn soldier or someone who pioneered uncharted territory or saved a life.

"Buzz! Agloobinflloff."

"I'm sorry? Say again?" I turned my good ear toward Amos, who usually kept his volume loud enough for me to hear. But I could make no sense of what he'd just said.

"Check it out. A slick car just pulled up." He pointed into the woods.

"How you can see anything through the trees is beyond me."

"No, look—on the other side of the bridge. It's parked."

Then, even I could see it. I placed a hand at my brow to shade my eyes. Out of the so-called slick car, a leg extended—a long one, attached to a short skirt. Not too short, just short enough. And out climbed an extraordinarily beautiful blonde.

Chapter 3

Emily

Whoa. The building to the west of the bridge, which apparently came attached to the property—was not much to look at. I peered in the windows. A pot-belly stove stood in the corner of the sole room. No electrical wires extended to the roof anywhere that I could see. There was a table, a ratty couch, a few metal-looking cabinets from what seemed like the Depression era, and—that was it.

Wow. Cabin living was accurate in the property listing's description. And I was the proud—or not-so-proud—owner of it now. How many mice lived inside? Gross.

Instead, I turned myself around and feasted my eyes on *the bridge*. Ta-da! A fanfare played in my ears—loud enough I expected a crown of glory to magically appear atop my head. I was the queen of what I surveyed, and I surveyed the prettiest covered bridge I'd ever beheld. Red facing walls framed either end—I walked across it to check—and the sides were open except for lattice-work along the sides, above the waist-high walls. It had a smooth, wood-slat floor, too.

It was perfect! I was in love! Tears formed, and the back of my throat got tight. It was even prettier in person than it had looked in the photos because I could see the vibrant green maple, oak, and spruce trees framing it, smell the evergreen balsam, and hear the brook that ran beneath it.

I'd heard of the term babbling brook, but I'd never actually *heard* a brook babble. Until now. Oh! Yeah! I threw my arms around myself and hugged hard. This was amazing, the best! It was better than catching any bouquet.

I pulled out my phone and took ten photos, twenty. Inside, outside, the brook, the west side, the east. The hills in the distance. I recorded the sound of my footfalls on the wood planks, noting the way it changed as I approached the edges versus the hollow echo of my steps in the middle.

Bridge, you and I are going to be on intimate terms.

I snapped ten more pictures—including a few selfies where I hugged one of the lattice-work posts.

Yes, it was ridiculously exuberant, but who cared? I owned a covered bridge! My life was pretty much complete.

"Uh, hello, lady." An older man, lanky and with a deeply lined face stood on the far side of the structure. "Are you all right? Do I need to call some kind of detox center for you to spend the night in? Our village of Maplebrook gots a drunk tank, if you want me to speak plain English at you."

"Um, hello." Why was it that whenever *I* danced like a crazy loon, someone had to be watching?

"The trusses are pretty impressive. I can see why you're photographing them." A different man walked up, but the sun shone from behind him, and all I could see was his form. A very nice form— pretty much an Adonis silhouette, if I were honest.

Not that I was looking for any reason other than to duly note it— since Justin more or less occupied my whole heart.

The Adonis looked up, exposing his Adam's apple. "The trusses were assembled in eighteen twenty-three, but the bridge itself was put up the next summer. The whole village of Maplebrook is mighty proud of our covered bridge."

So the town felt ownership, huh? Made sense. If I lived here, I would totally feel ownership over it, too. I'd think of it as mine.

Happily for me, it was! Title and all!

"You live here all your life?" I might as well be friendly with the natives. My cheeks flushed as this particular native stepped into the shadow where I could see his face. What a native!

Tall, with masculinity pouring off him, he wore his hair in one of those military flat-tops that I almost never saw anymore, at least not in Boston, but he wore it well. I caught a little sip of breath.

"I own Maplebrook Farm," he said. "It's adjacent to this property. I live in the house over there." He pointed through the bridge to the other side, where a much better looking farmhouse than mine sat. White clapboard, a steep-pitched roof, a wraparound porch, a proper chimney, an effusion of flowers hanging in planters out front, and a vegetable garden visible in the back yard. "I could show you the area. Are you thinking about moving to town?"

"Something like that." I should tell him I bought the bridge, but I wanted to get to know him first. That was a tactic I'd honed well in my business practices—feel out the competition. He might have been the other buyer with the offer on the table who I'd outbid. No sense making enemies right off the bat. "I'd love a tour of your farm, if you have time."

"Walk with me to Maplebrook Farm." Apparently, he had time. People out in the country must have gobs of time. Maplebrook Farm wasn't a farm-farm. "Maybe the name is a little misleading. First off, it's an orchard, not a farm."

We walked across the bridge, across his yard, and toward the tree-filled area. He held open a gate in a split-rail fence for me to cross into the orchard. He led the way, and I had to keep myself from letting my gaze slide toward his gait, toward his shoulder-to-hip ratio that seemed utterly golden. This guy could've been one of those Perfect Specimen types they based action figures on.

"What type of trees are in this orchard?" My image of an orchard was a dozen fruit trees. This was more like a hundred-acre wood.

"Sugar maples, almost exclusively, but some other varieties spring up occasionally."

Every inch was covered with green-leafed trees of varying heights, reaching for the skies. A true forest, it sat on a gently sloping hillside. Wind rustled the leaves, whispering that this was a place of peace.

"I'll bet the fall foliage is really something." I pictured the brilliant explosion of autumn colors that would overtake it in a few months. New England splendor, for sure.

"It shore is something!" The older fellow made this comment, and then he made an excuse that he needed to get back to work. "See you later, Buzz."

Time alone with the farmer named Buzz wasn't something I'd complain about.

Justin wouldn't mind.

After we'd traipsed up and down a little hill to see the view, Buzz took me on a meandering walking tour of his farm's sugar shack, where apparently in the winter, which was maple syrup season, they boiled down the sap. Maplebrook Farm produced a whopping two thousand gallons of syrup each year.

"How many gallons of sap make a gallon of syrup?" It couldn't be one-to-one. "Forgive me for knowing absolutely nothing about the maple business."

"Forty gallons of sap per gallon of syrup."

"Good grief! That's a lot of sap!" And he'd done two thousand gallons? "Just how many acres have you got here?" And how many trees? I couldn't even fathom!

He gave me some particulars of the business, and I soaked it up. It'd have to be murderous work in the cold to get that much sap in the first place, but wow, what a harvest. Thank you, Mother Nature!

"We're a throwback farm, too. We use a lot of the same techniques as developed in the nineteenth century—which are only mild updates over what the Iroquois used for collection in the pre-pilgrim days. Except we do have a reverse-osmosis evaporator to speed up the process."

The work seemed even more like scaling the Cliffs of Dover when he put it that way. "How do you survive?"

"It's hard work, but I've grown to love it. Keeps me connected to my family." He pulled a lopsided grin, like maybe he shouldn't have admitted something so personal to a stranger. "It's worth it."

My heart did a little flip. Good looking, hard-working, and on top of that—loyal to his family? If I weren't dating Justin, and if I didn't have a serious *life* back in Boston, I might end up chasing this orchard farmer.

But Justin was going to propose to me on my bridge.

"What more can you tell me about the bridge itself?" I asked. "Is it in use?"

The guy tilted his head and asked, "Can you repeat that?"

I repeated it, and then he answered, "It's only used by ATVs these days, or the occasional side-by-side." Those open vehicles. I knew them. "Nobody wants to damage it."

"Should it be reinforced?"

The lanky guy walked up at that moment, shouting, "No! Don't nobody gonna reinforce nothing on my bridge."

His bridge? As its neighbor, I could understand the ownership vibe.

"Amos, it appears, has strong feelings." Buzz smiled, and the sight caused my left knee to buckle.

I swear it was an involuntary reaction! Instead, I took note that the farmer's sidekick was named Amos. And that the handsome farmer treated him well, despite his quirks.

Also, that the handsome farmer was not wearing a wedding band.

I was not looking for that! I was not!

"I guess I'd better be getting back. Thank you for the tour." I left in

14

a hurry—before I could notice anything else about him, like whether he had very well-formed lips, or whether he had strong arms that might hold me nicely.

I was a mess. I revved my Mercedes's engine—probably a mirror for the chemistry revving in my veins—and then cut out of there, heading toward the village I'd passed through on my way.

There had to be at least one place to grab something to eat.

I pulled into the gravel parking lot of the only retail establishment I could see—The Furniture Store. It was a single-story building, sprawling wide, with just one display window—oddly, not offering furniture. Well, they could at least tell me where a girl could get a bite to eat.

A bell jingled on the door as I stepped into the dim, wood-paneled room. But, as the show window hinted, it didn't look to be selling much, if any, furniture. One wall had a refrigerator case with glass-front doors and shelves with milk and cheese. Another area carried hats, shirts, and boots. The far side looked like a school- and office-supplies store. But the granddaddy of it all was front and center: a glass deli case full of all kinds of delicious-looking foods.

My stomach growled to alert the world of my presence, and a woman in an apron appeared. "Welcome. Sounds like you need something to eat."

"I was expecting furniture, from the name of the store, but what a great surprise. That chicken sandwich looks just about right." It was the last one in the case, but it was chicken salad on a croissant, and the diced celery called to me with its crunchiness. "Could I also have one of those scones? Are they made in-house?"

She laughed, and it was like leaves rustling. "Sugar, the only option is in-house. In *my* house, which is attached to the back of the store." She laughed again and handed me the sandwich, after first wrapping it in fresh white wax paper. The crackle was amazing! I took it and it was all I could do not to take a deep whiff of its perfection. Then I received my scone, studded with cranberries. Oh, my. Country baking was my diet's nemesis. "Everyone around here has known this place as The Furniture Store for so long, no one thinks about the fact we don't sell much in the way of chairs or tables."

In walked a man who might be her husband. "Hey there." He tipped his hat to me. Tipped it! I could have died on the spot. Should I say out loud that I absolutely loved Maplebrook already? Even if I hadn't bought the covered bridge of my dreams in this place, this might be my dream town. "You new in town?" the hat-tipper asked.

"Sort of?" I took a bite of the sandwich, and it was salty, delicious heaven. I chewed and then swallowed. They waited patiently for my answer. "I bought the bridge."

"That was you! Well, welcome!" The lady's face split into a massive grin, like I'd just made her day. "We all wondered who'd snapped it up."

"Not Coolidge." The man gave a deep chuckle. "I'm Van, by the way. This is my wife, Greta. We own The Furniture Store. Third generation."

The family roots here went deep, it seemed. "Nice to see you."

We chatted a bit more, in which conversation I told them I was from Boston and loved the town so far. Then, I paid for my lunch, and as I turned to walk out, in through the jingling door burst a short man with a bristle-brush mustache.

"You two! If you ever get hold of whatever *witch* spelled that covered bridge out from under me, I expect you to tell me instantly!"

Decision point. Should I? Or should I dodge him?

Emily England did not dodge.

"I bought it." I rewrapped my sandwich and stuck out a hand. "Pleased to meet you. Name's England. Emily England."

"England! As in the country?"

It was like the first day of my seventh grade year all over again. "I should say it's France instead?" Which is what I'd resorted to as a thirteen-year-old.

Behind the deli counter, Van and Greta huff-laughed and then melted away.

"I'm Coolidge."

"Nice to have met you. See you later." I tried to step past him, but he lurched into my path, blocking my exit.

"If you think I'm just going to lie down and take this abuse, you have another think coming."

"Abuse!" Hardly. "I think you have the wrong person."

"You stole that bridge from me."

"I purchased it fair and square." And I'd read every line of the contract—a process I was used to in my everyday career. "I'm sorry you're upset."

"Upset! Upset doesn't begin to cover it." Foam formed at the edges of the bristle-brush. "If you think I'm going to just lie down, roll over, and let you steal what's rightfully mine, you have another think coming. I'm going to get that bridge, whether you like it or not."

People. I suppressed a tired sigh. I'd met excitable people like this Coolidge fellow too many times. "Legal title would disagree. Now, if you'll excuse me." I stepped past him, and soon I was in my car.

He pounded on my window, a small card in his hand.

Oh, brother. I opened it a crack. "Please, I don't want to run over your foot."

"Here. Take my card. When you're ready to sell, you'll call me." The card fluttered through the crack in the window and fell between the seat and the door frame. "If you don't, you'll have another think coming."

"Thanks, but no, thanks." I rolled up the window, closing the gap. "The covered bridge belongs to me," I said aloud, even though he couldn't hear.

As I peeled out of the lot and headed back toward Boston, a smile to match Greta's broke across my face. I owned a bridge! I couldn't wait to show Justin the pictures!

17

Chapter 4

Buzz

Summer nights came late at this latitude, and I had plenty of hours to work before true darkness fell. Crickets sang and grasses hissed in the breeze. I stayed hard at work.

"You didn't even drop your full name, bozo," Amos chided me later that night. "Or get hers."

"Hey. Who are you to call me a bozo?" And she'd heard Amos call me Buzz. Chances were, she'd assumed it was a nickname. Most people did. "Did it occur to you that was strategic?" I swung my hatchet harder. We were chopping wood from fallen branches we'd collected in the orchard and placing them in the woodpile for winter.

"Nope. It occurred to me it was boneheaded." More chuckling, a gurgling-like laugh. "You'll sure like having a beautiful neighbor. Her name's Emily, I heard. Emily France."

Emily. Well, I'd give Amos that—the woman had been beautiful— one of those pale-blonde petite girls with the light green eyes and confidence coming from every pore. "What do you mean, neighbor?" The woman had been passing through, admiring the bridge. "Tourist- type. That's it." Which was the sole reason I'd been able to keep it together while talking to her. Usually, I clammed up around any girl I met who was even the remotest date-possibility. *Because great girls deserved great guys. Guys like Neil, not bozos like me.*

"Turns out she was the buyer." Now Amos let out a full-blown guffaw. "Made Coolidge hopping mad. Don't know why he was in town—probably to try to stop the signing of the papers, but he was too late. Van told me everything."

Well, Van did hear everything and didn't mind sharing. Stuff that happened at The Furniture Store was considered public record.

"Let me remind you. You didn't tell her your name." Amos was not going to let this topic drop. I tried a few other subjects, but he was like a bulldog with it. "Don't worry, though. Van said she was heading back to the city. She did like the chicken salad on croissant."

Everyone liked Greta's chicken salad on croissant. "Gone, huh?" Bought the bridge and left. "Bad luck for us bachelors."

"If she comes back, I'm taking my shot." Amos pushed his hat farther back, revealing his ravine-filled brow. "Gorgeous woman. She might like a seasoned man."

Seasoned, as with too much garlic and onion. "Go for it."

I went back to chopping. The lack of full-name-exchange could've been subconsciously strategic. This way, she couldn't internet stalk me—not that she would, of course—and learn about my humiliation, or about my brother's catapult to fame, and feel sorry for me. Failed astronaut, the US Air Force survival school mishap, my plummet, Neil's rise to national stardom.

Yeah. She'd never have to know.

"Never mind." Amos loaded his arms with the wood and headed for the pile beside the sugar house that held our reverse osmosis system and the evaporator trays. "It was you, not me, she was a-looking at with wanton eyes."

"Wanton eyes! You gotta stop reading those historical romance novels at night, Amos. Wanton eyes." I scoffed.

But a tingle also ran from my toes to my scalp.

Me? She'd looked at me that way?

Chapter 5

Emily

Night fell as I rolled back into the tree-lined suburbs of Boston. An exceptionally long stoplight frazzled my nerves. I swear, traffic shortened my lifespan. Coming back from the mountains of Vermont, it'd been a long drive, but the day had gone swiftly while I toured Maplebrook Farm with that beefcake farmer.

Did anyone say *beefcake* these days? Probably not! However, there wasn't a better way to describe him. He'd alerted long-hibernating neurons in me, forcing them to stand up and salute. Somebody fan me. I dialed up my air conditioner a notch. Was it warm in here, or was it just my memory of Maplebrook Farmer's hotness?

Too bad I didn't get his name. I'd be internet stalking him at this stoplight.

Ooh, that was an idea. I whipped out my phone and went to the search bar—but bummer. A text notification popped up from Justin.

The *wrant-wrant-wrant* alarm of guilt sounded. I would have read it—to get Mr. Farmer out of my mind, but my email app chimed a notification from Mr. Pokoa.

For the moment, I was thankful for The Red Light of Eternal

Redness. I opened the message from the Big Boss and scrolled.

Subject line: *URGENT*. Wince. I stabbed it with my thumb and braced myself for the inevitable haranguing.

Instead of the usual lecture critical of me, or of my team's need to level-up our performance, however, the top line of the email—in all caps and bold type—read *EYES ONLY CONFIDENTIAL*. Was I being pulled into the boss's inner circle? And if so, why did heat crawl up my neck and bloom on my face? It should've felt great, not dreadful.

Honk! Honk! The light had changed, but I couldn't let this go unread. Not if it was urgent. Mr. P would want it read immediately.

Maneuvering like a pole position driver, and incurring more than my fair share of honking, I made my way to the side of the road and into the parking lot of the Green Burrito fast-food place, where I focused my eyes on my phone, scanning every word like a hungry tiger.

Data, data, more data. Then, I got to the meat of it, and tore in.

A deal likely to go bad with a merger in which *I'd* been the point person, the Gilsworth merger. An upcoming trade. A potential short sale? An exorbitant sum listed ...

Just a second! This wasn't a warning.

This was *an invitation to commit a crime*: insider trading.

All the blood drained from my head. Faint, I was going to faint or be sick. This was so wrong. Why would Mr. Pokoa send this to me? Why hadn't I heard about any of it before now? And was I unwittingly complicit?

A million pounds of bad cheese filled my senses.

I shut off my car, got out to pace and think. I set the phone on top of my Mercedes like it was a grenade with the pin pulled—backing away slowly and then turning and crouching like I needed to cover my head before the explosion.

This had to be a mistake. What was today's date? April first? Was this an April Fool's Day joke? No, the calendar was closer to the end of summer, and the email's tone hadn't felt jokey at all, unless I was misreading it. Gingerly, I made my way back to the car and the ticking time bomb of a message, perusing it more carefully this time.

No, it didn't get better. In fact, it got exponentially more disgusting. My ears roared. I should call Justin and warn him.

But before I did, I checked in the *recipients* line on the email.

Justin's name was listed.

Oh, heavens. Oh, nightmares.

Who could help me figure out my next move? I needed counsel.

I walked around to take deep breaths of the car-exhaust-filled air of Boston.

My toe tapped on the hot asphalt while I stewed, but a text chimed.

Instinct made me check it. Justin. This time I opened it.

Hey, if you by chance get an email marked URGENT from Pokoa today, just dismiss it. It was sent to you by accident.

I read the text a few times. Justin, my boyfriend, my paragon of virtue and integrity, didn't want me opening the email because …

It couldn't be what it looked like! It looked like he was covering for our boss.

Or worse, he was complicit with the boss.

No. Just no. There had to be an explanation. I racked my brain for some way he could be innocent in this. *It's insider trading!* Insider trading is wrong. Justin had to be innocent!

I dialed his number, but my call went to voice mail.

The parking lot's asphalt was still hot. I could feel it through the soles of my shoes if I stood still, so I went over to the curbing near a tree. A few things Justin had said lately—things about future profits, about a *sure thing*—roared into my brain.

Worst of all, they were using *my* merger as the dirty deal.

I picked up a piece of gravel from the landscaping and hurled it hard at the ground. It ricocheted and hit my tire.

The space between my eyes pinched. More memories of Justin's recent behavior trickled in—late nights with the boss, secret meetings, his insisting *I* be the one to run the Gilsworth merger, monologues about loyalty that I'd thought so charming and valiant at the time. Now

22

I could see them for what they were—loyalty among thieves.

Loyalty!

What about integrity?

What about his loyalty to me? The backs of my eyes stung.

I dialed again, but not Justin. My dad's former attorney Jerry McCormick came on the line.

"Nice to hear from you, Emily." Jerry sounded chipper. He had helped Dad, despite the fact Dad had been guilty as sin, and had counseled Dad to change his ways.

"Hey, Jerry. I've got a … situation."

Jerry took my story over the phone. I blatted all the details through the ether at him, trying to keep a quaver out of my voice.

Finally, I asked, "What is the smart move here, Jerry? My merger is the core of the scheme." Jerks! Jerkfaces! Hideous wretches! I ran out of names to call them. "I haven't done anything wrong."

"But they'll make it look like you have."

No kidding. I paced beside my car. *Do not hyperventilate in the Green Burrito parking lot. Do not pass out in the Green Burrito parking lot.*

"Don't go to the office."

No kidding. "Right. So? What should I do instead?"

"It's possible I can get you a plea deal if you turn state's evidence. You do know the Securities and Exchange Commission will be coming after you."

Yep. I knew. Years ago, Dad had been their target—and rightfully so—when I was a kid. "They aren't lenient."

"They may be. Forward me the email. I'll do my best for you. In the meantime, mail me that phone, and get a different one with a new number. Do you have anywhere you can stay? Somewhere out of town, somewhere they wouldn't be able to find you and—"

"You think my boss and coworkers will retaliate?" That seemed so unthinkable!

"You're turning them in, I assume."

I was definitely turning them in. I didn't even need to ponder compromising my integrity. Ugh! My friends, coworkers, my *boyfriend*. How could they betray me like this: compromise their integrity—and put mine in jeopardy? We'd worked long days and into the nights together, ordering Boston Cream Pie as celebrations after big wins. I genuinely liked them. They liked me, too. *I might have even fallen for Justin—married him—given the right moments.* "They've been my friends. They wouldn't come after me for revenge."

"From what I know about Pokoa through other sources, there's potential nastiness, if not outright danger."

Danger! "You're being serious, Jerry."

"I am." He listed a few local rumors.

They were not good.

How could I have been working with them all this time and not seen?

This was the worst.

Moreover, I needed a cave to crawl into—somewhere away from Justin, away from all the men I shouldn't have ever relaxed my vigilance around and trusted.

"I'm serious about disappearing, Emily."

"I do have a primitive option." Complete with a few friendly mice. "Yeah, I mean, I have somewhere." Somewhere they'd never been to visit or seen. I'd pay ahead on my Boston rent, and then … disappear into Vermont. "I'll be in touch with my new number soon."

"Emily? Good luck. Doing the right thing is almost always the rockier road."

Yeah. My best day just morphed into my worst.

Before dropping my phone into the mail to Jerry for safekeeping, though, I did send one final text—to Justin, my fingers shaking to match the quiver in my chin.

I've been thinking. We've grown apart too much. It's not going to work out between us. Thanks for the memories. The fake ones, where I'd thought he was a hero.

24

Bitter tears escaped the sides of my eyes. How could they? How could *he?* When he *knew* how much being upright and honest meant to me! It stabbed my heart time after time.

Turns out my hero is a villain.

Chapter 6

Buzz

The sun peeked over the trees as a snorting truck disturbed my breakfast. It rattled over the road on the other side of the bridge from Maplebrook Farm. Another bridge fanatic doing a drive-by? Too loud for that, with all the door slamming and such. It was audible even over the creek's rumble.

I cleared breakfast away and headed across the bridge to inspect the cause of the racket.

What? Emily? The gorgeous blonde from yesterday? *The woman who'd bought the bridge?* I'd never expected to see her again. She'd been so … *city.*

My step hesitated a moment, but then I straightened and approached. Emily today wore jeans and a work shirt, and she'd tied her pale blonde hair up in a high ponytail.

I called to her as I walked up. "You were so charmed by the attractions of this little house you had to move in the very next day?"

"I'm not one for delays." She climbed into her truck's bed, though there didn't seem to be much room for her. Too many crates and chairs.

"Where'd your slick car go? I'm using Amos's description of it, by the way."

"I traded my slick car for this truck." She dragged a cardboard

26

moving box to the tailgate. "It's better suited to country living."

No doubt, but—"Correct me if I'm wrong, but something led me to believe yesterday that you weren't planning on country living." Nor was she suited for it, considering the gear she'd brought. Everything in her truck looked high-end, way too city-chic for the ramshackle shack it was destined to decorate. "You sure you want to put this nice leather armchair in that place? Or these nice linen drapes? Your house, shall we call it, sits at the edge of a field, and ..."

The unspoken word *mice* hung between us.

"Yes. But you're right if you're saying I'm not prepared to live in that house. I mean, I've never been camping or anything."

"I'm sorry?" I hadn't quite heard what she said. "What did you say?"

"That my dad never took me camping," she repeated a little louder. "So, my new digs have *Emily's Big Adventure* written all over them."

No! "Your dad never took you camping?" Criminal! "What was wrong with him?"

"He was too busy."

"Doing what? No dad should be too busy to take his kids camping."

She frowned. "He was unavoidably detained."

Could she possibly mean jail?

I mouthed the word. It clunked between us, squashing the mice.

She mashed her mouth to one side and nodded.

"Got it. Which means exactly one thing." I pushed her nice leather armchair back into the bed of the pickup, beside a velvet-upholstered ottoman. "You're not ready for this place."

"You can't make me go back to Boston. I own the property."

"That's not what I mean." I closed the tailgate like it was an exclamation point. "I mean, you can't live in it. It's not ready for you."

"Trust me, I'm strong. I can do anything I set my mind to."

"Can you go without a hot shower and use an outhouse? What about without Wi-Fi?"

Her cute nose wrinkled. "You're kidding."

"I wish I were."

She huffed a long sigh and crumpled against the truck, sitting on the bumper. "Cold showers I can do—and *definitely* I can live without Wi-Fi—but nighttime trips outside when nature calls? I don't really want to traipse through nature." She looked up at the sky, as if to question *why me* and then back at me, the light gone from her face. "Got any suggestions?"

"Just one."

"Yeah?" A tiny brightness returned to her pale green eyes. "What is it?"

"Swap me houses." Okay, I know—this was ridiculous and risky and beyond the call of duty. By a million miles. And it might've even seemed like I was a creeper. But it was also my chance to make a pretty woman's day. Maybe even her year.

"Swap. With you?"

"We passed my place yesterday." I aimed a thumb at it. "Farmhouse, porch, big trees, white siding."

"I know the house." She clearly wasn't sold. "Across the bridge, not a quarter of a mile off."

"An eighth of a mile, to be exact, with only the Maple Brook between the two places."

"And where would you be?" The skepticism dripped.

"I'd live in your place, do a little construction for hire, and you'd rent mine in the meantime." I was gallant, but I also wasn't a pushover about funds. Besides, she seemed like the type of woman who'd definitely want to pay her fair way.

"You'd do that for me?" Her eyes narrowed. "Do you have any construction experience?"

"Not formally, but I'm a farmer." I shrugged noncommittally. They'd taught us to be resourceful in the military, too. "Farmers have to figure things out every single day. I built the addition to a shed over at my house." And we'd attempted a tree house, Dad and I.

For a second, she still hesitated. "And … what's the catch?"

She seemed like she was used to catches, like she'd been reading the fine print all her life.

"No catch." I shrugged. "You might not trust me at first sight, but you can ask Amos. You can ask anyone. I'm not a jerk. I keep my word. If I mess up on the house—"

"Mess it up? It can't exactly get worse messed up than it is."

"Right?"

Suddenly she looked fragile, tired, and beaten. "Forgive me for sounding skeptical."

"I get it. You don't know me at all." I held open my hands. "I might mess up. I might cost you some money. I might let you down."

Her mouth formed a line. She'd been let down—it was clear as day.

"Your offer is generous. Beyond generous. In fact, you might be the most generous neighbor I've ever heard of."

Until I die, I will never know what gave me the nerve to do what I did next.

But I, Buzz Atchison, took this stranger in my arms. "It's going to be okay, Emily. You can trust me."

By rights, she should have shoved me away. Slapped me, even. Instead, she collapsed against me, filling my senses with her perfume.

It lasted a long moment—though not long enough for me.

"I guess people hug in the country." She pulled out of my arms, then put her hands in her back pockets.

"They don't hug in the city?" Thinking of my years in the city—no. Not that much hugging.

"Not people they just met."

To be honest, there also wasn't a tremendous amount of hugging in Maplebrook, either. *I'm kicking off a trend.* Well, I wouldn't mind a trend. The hug lingered like a phantom against my chest. I might never shake it. *I want that again.*

Emily wiped her forehead, took a deep breath, and then said, "I'll pay for all the upgrades, make sure none of it comes out of your pocket. I'll pay any rent you ask."

See? I'd read her correctly. "Naturally."

"But—do you have time to do this?"

"Most guys with maple syrup businesses spend their off-seasons tagging trees for future taps and bow-hunting on the side."

"Bow-hunting!"

Hunting was very big among guys with my profession. "It's not maple season yet. I've got time."

A sucker with a lot of time. Emphasis on sucker. I didn't even know whether she was single. Tell you what, I was thinking with something other than my logical engineer's brain when I struck this deal. I'd been mesmerized by her enthusiasm for ditching Wi-Fi. Yeah, that was it.

By evening, we'd scrawled illegible signatures across the bottom of a rental contract. Her furniture and other items were safely ensconced in my place, and all of my necessities had been moved to the trash hut on the other side of the bridge, along with some food and blankets. It was going to be mighty cold with only a pot-belly stove as soon as the first freeze hit upper Vermont in a few weeks, so I'd have to work fast. Good thing Amos and I had cut and stacked a nice woodpile.

"How can I repay you?" Emily France leaned against the doorframe of my farmhouse, her hair now down and spilling across her shoulders. "I don't mean in money, because that's all settled with my rent, but I mean in time. You're giving time—and I should, too."

"An orchard guy can always use help with taps when the season hits."

"Taps, as in tapping the trees for sap?"

"Sure."

"I'd love to try. Of course, you'd be taking a risk on me. I don't even know what a sugar maple looks like."

"Turnabout is fair play. You're taking a risk on hiring a farmer as your home renovation contractor."

"Okay, but this is your livelihood. You'd have to train me."

And spend more time with Emily France? "Consider it done."

"When is maple season?"

"Generally February or early March. Depends on the weather." When nights were freezing and days were above freezing for several days in a row, the sap ran best and sweetest. "You staying that long?"

A dark cloud—like an absorption nebula from the darkest part of space—passed over her face. "Through the winter." It passed, but it left me wondering about what mystery she hid.

"You're really something, Buzz. It's an unusual name. It's your legal name?" She'd seen it on the contract.

"Yeah. My actual given name." I'd heard a million times how weird it was. Don't even get me started on that movie with the toy cowboy and the toy spaceman.

"Is the name a reflection of your haircut—or the reverse?"

"This happens to be a flat-top, not a buzz." I grazed my hand across the top of my vestigial-military-service haircut. "My dad likes astronaut names." And astronauts.

"Very cool. You're built like an astronaut." She gave me a once-over.

To my credit, I didn't blush—or even push my shoulders back and walk like one of those jocks near the high school locker room. "Thanks?"

"It's a compliment. You're welcome." She scratched the side of her nose. "See you tomorrow."

"Tomorrow?"

"Sure, to go shopping for supplies to fix the Gilligan's Island hut you just willingly moved into."

"And you'll need some groceries. My cupboard is pretty bare."

"Thanks for leaving the bread and peanut butter, though." Her gaze went to the horizon. "Buzz?"

"Yeah?"

"Can I ask you a random question? It's philosophical."

31

Huh. "Okay. Shoot."

She continued looking out into the distance. "Do you think integrity is more abundant among those who live in the country than it is among those who live in the city?" She turned to me, and her breath caught—almost as if how I answered this question mattered more than anything else in the world to her in this moment.

I pondered. My neck itched.

"Never mind," she said, holding up a hand. "Sleep on it and tell me your answer tomorrow."

Tomorrow. I'd see her tomorrow. "See you tomorrow." I jumped off the porch and headed toward the bridge—walking just like one of those high school jocks near the locker room.

Chapter 7

Emily

I walked around and explored the house I'd been given. Not to be nosy, but … I lived in Buzz's place now. I needed to know my way around. *And to know the guy I'd trusted—tentatively.*

And not just because he'd hugged me and made me feel safer than I'd felt in days.

It was a smallish farmhouse, three bedrooms and a bathroom. Not primitive, but certainly not city-standard modern. The wraparound porch made it feel bigger.

His decorating theme landed somewhere between man-cave and practical-farmer's den. He'd taken his sole frying pan and cook pot with him, but he'd left most everything else. In some ways it was homey. Photos of New England landscapes, a wall-size topographical map of his orchard, and a family photo—with Buzz, two people who must be his parents, and another guy who looked a lot like Buzz—were on the walls. Thick rugs covered the hardwood floors. My leather sofa dominated the living room, but a vintage wooden rocking chair held a place in the corner.

And the books! Books make a home. He had an interesting collection—everything from math textbooks to Robert Frost poetry. In this New England setting, Frost made a lot of sense. I took it off the shelf and thumbed through the pages, stopping for a moment on "Stopping by Woods on a Snowy Morning."

How would this white clapboard farmhouse with the pitched clay-shingle roof look under a blanket of snow? Idyllic. *I can't wait for the fall colors.*

Yeah, considering his books and everything, I was probably all right trusting Buzz Atchison with my ... well, with my building project at the least.

At ten or so, I walked across the bridge to meet Buzz.

"Remind me. How far is it from here into town?" I asked as I climbed into his much-nicer-than-mine pickup truck. "I can't remember, even though I was just there yesterday." A lot had happened since then.

"The village is four miles." He started up and we drove down the road.

"Is The Furniture Store really the only place to get groceries within twenty miles?" I'd been there yesterday, met the owners.

"That's what makes it the hub of Maplebrook. Everybody's gotta eat." He slowed for a deer looking to cross the road. "They also have plumbing supplies, lumber, sheetrock, and so forth. We'll probably need to go quite a few times during the process of remodeling your place."

"Okay," I said. "Sounds good. About my question from last night ..." Would he even remember I'd asked it? "You have an answer for me yet?" I asked.

He looked up. "Come again?"

Either he'd forgotten or else he hadn't heard me now. I dialed down the fan on the truck's loud air conditioner. "Have you thought about what I asked last night? About whether integrity is more prevalent among people in the country than in the city."

He nodded but didn't turn toward me as he answered. "I've been chewing on it."

So, he'd been thinking. "And?" *And everything hinges on how he answers.*

It was a ridiculous litmus test, I know, but after Dad and Justin—I just needed to know how he felt on this topic, the topic of integrity. People who saw good people around them were often good themselves.

Meanwhile, the two men I'd been closest to in my entire life, to whom I'd given all my trust, had both decimated it in an instant. Even after learning my lesson from Dad, that integrity is a commodity only valuable to a few, I'd been charmed by Justin and his flattering words. False words.

Forgive me if I was a little off, a little slow to let go of the iron fist that clamped shut the box containing my trust.

"And?" Buzz said. "The truth is, city or country, uprightness as location-centered ... I'm not sure."

"Because you've only experienced the country life?" The hot morning had created a haze floating over the trees, like the haze of worry in my mind.

"Didn't I tell you?" The truck slowed as we turned a sharp bend in the tree-lined road. "I've only been running Maplebrook Farm for about seven years. It belonged to my great-uncle, and to my great-grandfather before that."

He'd told me that much. "What were you doing before?"

"I worked in Concord."

"That's right near Boston!" I was master of the obvious. But it shocked me that I'd been so close to him in the past. "We could have run into each other at some point."

"Not sure. Did you hang out in aeronautical engineering firms?"

"Not regularly." Or ever. "You're an engineer?" He didn't look like an engineer. He looked like an Olympian. Or ... an astronaut. His name made that connection. "Did it not take?"

"It didn't take." His temples pulsed, and his eyes were trained straight ahead.

Something had happened to this guy in Concord, or some other time or place to this guy to bring him to Maplebrook. What could it have been?

"Anyway, I'm here in Maplebrook now, and the country people I associate with mostly seem honest. There are some exceptions, but I've met good people in both places. My guess is that my former coworkers at Uffern Engineering were too busy crunching numbers and writing code that would improve airplanes to think up any kind of nefarious schemes or hatch corrupt plots, so as far as I know, I wasn't really in contact with people who didn't have integrity. Still, I don't think it's geographically based."

"Huh. Maybe not." Wise points, though, about career choice and integrity. I'd have to think about those later. Right now, however, I got sidetracked because I pictured him in a shirt and tie, sitting at a desk making trigonometric calculations. Imaginary engineer-Buzz was pretty attractive, too.

"Did I answer to your satisfaction?"

As a matter of fact, he had—but not exactly how he perhaps thought. In my experience, people who proclaimed that *everyone is corrupt* or *everyone lies in court* were likely the type who were corrupt and who lied in court, and who likely surrounded themselves with birds of a feather. The fact that Buzz's experience had been mostly with honest people who were doing their daily jobs, pushing forward, led me to believe that he, too, was upstanding and honest.

It was a strong clue to his character, though I wasn't ready to invest my full emotional trust at this point. I'd learned my lesson too many times. Twice bitten, ten times shy. But I could at least trust that he'd uphold a contract, that he wasn't out to harm me physically.

"I heard this isn't your first trip to The Furniture Store." Buzz pulled into the gravel parking lot. "Amos said you'd met Van and Greta already."

Amos. I hadn't figured him for the town gossip, but the shoe might fit. "They seem great. She makes a very good scone."

"And an excellent chicken salad sandwich on croissant." He pulled into the parking lot.

Oh, brother. So the gossip extended to what I'd ordered at the deli counter? Good grief. Country living was like everything else—a two-sided coin. I'd have to take the good with the bad.

"Emily, you're back." Greta greeted us when we entered the dim store. While my eyes adjusted, I smiled and stood still, so as not to go bumping around into any of the million displays filling the space. "Didn't expect to see you so soon. Or with our local bachelor, Buzz Atchison."

"The local bachelor?" I asked, eyeing him.

"Amos and I are famous for the status," he said with a shrug, "but he's more likely to end his bachelor status than I am."

"Oh, really?" I tried to probe, but he jumped deep into selecting copper tubing, a hot water heater, and all the rest of our initial needs for the renovation.

Finally, we had collected a genuine haul, and Van helped us get it all out to Buzz's truck. It nearly filled the bed, and I'd spent quite a bit of the cash surplus from trading my Mercedes for my current jalopy.

"Mind if I stop by the post office?" He drove us in the opposite direction of Maplebrook Farm and my bridge. "You're probably thinking about setting yourself up a post office box here, aren't you?"

Nope. I didn't want any breadcrumbs for them to follow. "Sometime, maybe. Not today."

"All right. But I still need to stop in." He parked in front of the low, brick building flanked by flame-red bushes and alighted, motioning for me to follow him in. "You should at least come in and meet Rosie. She's Amos's sister."

Amos and Rosie? We went inside, where stood a bright-eyed woman with crags that matched the deep lines on her brother's face. Her white hair flew out everywhere from the loose bun atop her head, and she came out from behind the counter and threw her arms around Buzz.

"Buzz!" She pressed her cheek to his chest, barely coming up to

37

his armpit in height. "You dear boy. Amos says you've been making stew and force-feeding it to him."

"Guilty."

"Well, I thank you. He won't eat anything I cook." She let him go and returned to her post. "Now, box one-oh-nine, who's your friend? She's very pretty. No one told me you'd gone off and eloped."

Buzz reached across the counter and took both of Rosie's hands. "How could I do that when you're my best girl?" The guy could flirt. "This is my new neighbor, Emily France. She bought the covered bridge."

I hiccuped—first at the fact he was such a flirt, and I did not trust flirts. Second at his use of the wrong last name for me. For a moment, I opened my mouth to correct him, but then I clamped it shut, and just smiled.

Being Emily France to everyone in Maplebrook instead of Emily England while I was here in hiding may just work to my advantage.

"Good for you, dearie." Rosie bestowed a smile on me. "We all thank you for buying it up before you-know-who could."

I probably did know who. "It's a dream come true for me."

Buzz turned to me. "Is that right? How so?"

Uh, I wasn't about to go spilling my guts to him right now about my lifelong dream of being kissed and proposed to on a bridge. Or about how Justin had thrashed that dream to chaff in the last forty-eight hours. "Just a childhood wish."

Before Buzz could press me further—and he looked as if he would—Rosie asked me about my postal needs. "Will you be wanting a personal-size box, or would you need more of a business size? You look rather like someone who runs a business to me."

"I give off that vibe, huh?" For the first time in what seemed like forever, I laughed out loud. I'd arranged to forward all my mail to Jerry anyway, just to be safe. "Good to know. But I am not expecting to receive much mail. I'll just take delivery at home."

Rosie and Buzz exchanged glances and said nothing.

"What?" I asked. "Isn't that an option?" This was America, after all. The US Postal Service was legendary for their whole sleet and dark of night motto.

"We're rural, honey. There's no rural postal home delivery in a village this size."

Good grief. "Okay." I tried to recover quickly from my obvious gaffe. "My city-girl is showing. I'll figure things out and get back with you about renting a box, I guess." Or not. If I didn't have a postal address, I was less likely to be found.

Better, I didn't live in the house on the property I owned. Chances were, I could be very difficult to trace.

"I'll just go pick up my things from the box and meet you in the truck." Buzz went out of the window area to the lobby where the boxes were, but Rosie detained me.

"Emily? Can you stay a sec?"

"Okay." I paused, my hand on the metal frame of the glass door. "Something wrong?"

"Nope. I just want to tell you that Buzz is one of the good ones."

Had she read my mind, or heard my unspoken question from while I was riding over to town with him? "What makes you say that?" I always wanted specifics when someone made a general assertion.

"If you can't see it, I can't tell you." Rosie frowned at me for a moment, as if to reinforce her statement. "So, *see* well."

The words quaked in me, hairline-cracking the thick ice layer that had formed around my soul to keep out men like Justin. "I'll try."

I met Buzz in the truck. My heart sparked with imagination when he handed me a lump of something wrapped in white wax paper. "Chicken salad on a croissant okay? Greta brought them over."

"You dreamboat!" I opened it. "These are divine, by the way. Thanks." I took a scrumptious mouthful. "What about you?"

"I ate mine while you were talking with Rosie. It only took me three bites." His statement sent my eyes darting toward his broad shoulders. "Rosie's a smart woman. She's good to her brother."

Buzz was good to Rosie's brother, too, it seemed.

And to me.

The guy collected Robert Frost poetry, which told me something else about him, that he liked to think about nature and people and life.

He might be a lot of other good things, too. I'd take Rosie's advice and try to *see*, as she'd insisted.

I'd seen a lot already. Buzz was funny, sharp, kind—but not to a fault. Now and then, I saw an undercurrent of sadness in him. Had something happened to him? Something had happened to nearly everyone. The walking wounded—we all had something. I had Dad—and now Justin.

What was Buzz's secret?

Then there were his laid-back ways. Talk about refreshing! After life in Boston among the driven, self-absorbed, do-anything-to-win types. Buzz was … clean air after breathing pollution.

Speaking of breathing, mmm. The air conditioning wafted his cologne at my senses. I closed my eyes and luxuriated in the scent, which brought the memory of the way his arms had felt wrapped around me, holding me against the storms of the day.

He was a shelter.

Buzz felt safe. Real. Moored and anchored and rooted.

Someday, I might even tell him why I bought the bridge near his sugar maple farm.

The trees blurred as we sped past them. Everything was going to be all right—at least for a while.

Chapter 8

Buzz

A week of home improvement projects, and I'd been with Emily most of every single day. She'd insisted on helping out.

"It's the blind leading the blind," I said, but for some reason, I wasn't the least bit worried about it.

"Everything can be figured out," she'd said. And then, she'd had to witness me messing things up like welding the copper piping wrong the first three times, until she'd looked up the DIY video for me and we'd watched it together—twice. Finally, we'd gotten her hot water heater installed.

Despite several incidents like that, she'd stayed sunny and determined through all of them. And she hadn't made me feel dumb about it. It was like we were a team, not like I was her hired hand.

Of course, the installation of the hot water heater had been a top priority, since it meant I'd be the lucky guy finally taking hot showers from now until the place was ready for Emily to move in. I wasn't dumb.

On the other hand, being around her day in and day out was getting me to the point where cold showers might become a necessity. Merciful heavens above. The woman was killing me with that walk, the way those sweaters fit her, the jeans that hugged her hips when she handed me a pipe wrench or wire cutters.

And then, when she took over and figured out the wiring situation in the bedroom we were building her, I could have run a hundred miles and still not cooled down.

But I wasn't making any kind of move. We were neighbors. If things went sour, the proximity could be awkward. Forever. As for me, I wasn't planning on moving away from Maplebrook Farm—ever. And the woman loved her bridge to distraction. Man, the way she'd danced on it that first day! Sexy as all get-out.

Okay, that might have been the first day I sort of fell for her. At least—if I had been the type to fall for someone. Which I wasn't.

Since I wasn't the type that they fell for in return.

"What made you buy Maplebrook Farm?" Emily asked as we dangled our feet off the porch of my farmhouse while eating corn on the cob—the last of this year's crop from my not-too-impressive vegetable garden. "I mean, I know it was in the family, but you had a job in Boston."

"Concord."

"Stop dodging the point."

Nailed. "If you really want to know"—I set the empty cob down and wiped my face with a napkin while I debated how much to tell and how much to edit—"my dad grew up here. His grandparents raised him. He worked the orchard with them every winter, went to school in Maplebrook, and this was home for him. When it looked like it might pass out of the family after Great-Uncle Walter passed away …"

"You played the family hero."

"Hero! Me?" A deep gurgle rose up my throat. "Hardly. If you want hero, that's my brother, Neil."

"Neil, as in the other astronaut?"

"The *actual* astronaut. I'm sure you've heard of him." By now, she would have at least done a cursory internet search to find out who I was,

42

and it would have led her straight to Neil. Every woman I'd ever met had done so. Emily would be no different. I braced myself, probably gripping the wood slats on the porch too tightly.

"This may come as a surprise to you," she said, "but I'm a hundred percent ignorant of any astronauts' by name—at least any after that tragic incident in the eighties with the Challenger explosion," she said.

"Christa McAuliffe," I supplied. "School teacher, though. Not an astronaut, per se."

"But your brother is? Is that cool? Especially if you were also studying aeronautics? How is that for you?"

My fingers loosed their boards. In the ten years since the series of semi-tragic events that separated Neil's path from mine, all anyone had ever wanted to talk about was Neil, his experience. The heroism. For the first time, someone—a beautiful woman—asked about me.

For that reason, I was totally unprepared. It would take care for me to formulate the right response, so I put it on the back burner. "I'll tell you about it. Sometime."

"All right." She didn't push. She just took another bite of her corn. "I, for one, am glad you're keeping this farm in your family."

"Thanks." Maybe, someday, Dad would be glad, too—that is, if I was able to make the balloon payment, come the end of this calendar year. "I'm working at it."

***

A few mornings later, I left Emily and her soldering iron and copper wires at the Bridge Cottage, as we were now calling it, and made the trek to town alone.

A dreaded trek. And it had to be sans Emily.

"Lo and behold." Yves jumped to his feet as soon as I entered the farm loan office and pumped my hand. "If it isn't Buzz Atchison. Are you here about the loan? I guess you got my letters."

I'd gotten them all right, the whole stackola of them. "I thought I'd bring in my monthly payment in person this time."

"Sit down, sit down." Yves seated me in a chair across from him at his old, polished curly maple desk. "How is the syrup business going at Maplebrook Farm? I read in the almanac we may have a very odd freezing pattern this year."

"Good to know." The almanac? Who put stock in that these days? The same people who went to fortunetellers, probably. Although, the local almanac had been eerily correct about that freak weather event the news called a *bomb cyclone* about five years ago. "I'm putting in about a thousand more taps this year, if Amos is on his toes."

"Two hundred fifty more gallons of syrup? That translates into ..."

"Enough to make the balloon payment." I nudged him. "But not until after the syrup season."

"Which is, to my reckoning, three or four months after your payment is due." A new frown replaced all Yves's bright smiles. "You knew this when you signed."

"But you'd get your money back. It's guaranteed."

"I can't alter the details of the loan repayment schedule, Buzz."

Balloon payments should be illegal. They were immoral at the minimum. "It's just a few weeks' difference."

Instead of arguing with me, Yves reached into his drawer and pulled out a bright orange flier. He pushed it across the table toward me. "This may be of interest to you."

I scanned it. "A protest meeting?"

"Yes, against a new sawmill proposed for the area." Yves laced his fingers across his broad belly as if he'd solved all my problems. "The meeting should tell you everything you need to know."

"Why don't you tell me some of the things?" Since he seemed to know them. "The meeting is still a ways off."

"Locals supposedly want to put a stop to it, but a sawmill from Burlington is seeking to expand. They'll put in a mill somewhere near here along Maple Brook, and rumor has it anyone who wants to sell an orchard early will get a premium."

Cut down my orchard! "I'm not doing that."

"Did you hear the word *premium*, Buzz? They're paying top dollar for stands of trees they can contractually secure ahead of time. It might not even be that they'll cut them for a while. You can keep your land and have your money too. Why not simply plant more maples once what you have is cleared out? They do grow back, you know."

In forty years. It takes forty—not fourteen, not four—years for a maple to mature to the point where it can be tapped. My ire flowed like sap after a freeze. I decided I'd better leave before it burst through one of my poorly plugged taps. "Thanks for the information." I headed to the door.

"You forgot your flier!" Yves called.

No, I hadn't. He chased me and shoved it into my pocket.

I wadded it and shoved it deeper.

Cutting down the orchard would be so much worse than simply losing it to the bank. I could picture Dad now. *You chopped down Maple Brook Farm's entire orchard?* Even the imaginary disappointment curdled my soul.

I'd seen enough disapproval from Dad in the past. If only I could accomplish something big enough that I could rid Dad of his shame of me for good. Forever.

Selling all the trees would be the opposite of that.

Maplebrook Farm is my one chance. My last chance. I had to figure out a way to make that balloon payment. Especially now that I knew if I couldn't pay and the orchard went up for sale, whoever bought it next would probably be tempted to sell out to the Burlington sawmill people with their attractive offers and contracts.

I couldn't let that happen.

I sped back to Maplebrook Farm. When I lurched into the driveway of my old place—I'd gone there out of thoughtless habit—Emily met me on the porch of the farmhouse with a sandwich and that incredible smile of hers, the thoughtfulness almost curing my pain.

"I thought you were never coming back. I made you something."

I wasn't hungry, even though she'd gone to the trouble of fixing something for me to eat. "I'm just going for a walk in the orchard." To

45

cool off. Since, obviously, the drive back from the village hadn't worked. At all.

"Can I come with you?"

To my sanctuary where I needed to escape and process all my unmet expectations? I should say no. "Okay." Since the first minute I saw her, I hadn't been able to resist any request.

I waited for the thirty seconds it took for her to pull on her boots. I needed to stomp through the trees alone and think, but something had made me let Emily tag along. *The something being my testosterone that couldn't resist the requests of a beautiful woman who could wield a soldering iron.*

"You said you'd teach me about the trees." Huffing a little with exertion, Emily met my pace, stride for stride.

"Right." I realized I was moving like I was in one of those forced marches we'd had to do during my Air Force training camp days, and I curbed my pace's enthusiasm, slowing down to match her gait.

"We've been so busy remodeling the Bridge Cottage that it just hasn't happened yet. But I want to know everything about the trees. Like, are these all maples? Are they all sugar maples? How do you grow them? How old are they?"

"Slow down." I almost laughed. "You'll choke me on the fire-hose flow." We climbed over the split-rail fence that Great-Uncle Walter had built to delineate the family yard from the orchard property.

"I'm serious, Buzz. And I'm a quick study. Just lay it on me."

So, I did.

"You can recognize a sugar maple by its gray-brown, almost shaggy bark. The leaves are darker green on the top side than the bottom. The leaves have five lobes, and they look like the Canadian flag."

"How many of these are sugar maples?"

"All these are sugar maples." I waved my hand indicating all the trees around us. "Over time, the caretakers have removed the other trees and only left this variety—which is why my great-grandpa called it a

farm. They were all planted from seed, since maples don't graft well, but many are from long before the Atchison family's time as owners of the property."

"How much before?"

"Oh, my dad told me once that several trees that we regularly tap were standing during the Civil War."

Emily halted in her tracks. She grabbed my forearm and stopped me, as well. "You're kidding." Her touch radiated up my arm.

"Not kidding. In fact, maples can live to be three hundred years old. So, yeah. A few in this forest might be older than our country itself."

Emily left off touching me, stretched her arms out, her eyes wide, and she spun in a slow circle. "This is better than touring a cathedral in Europe." When she stopped, she looked at me, still alive with wonder. "There's a connection to the past here that I never knew about."

"Uh-huh." So true. To my own family's past—and beyond that. "I totally agree."

Without warning, Emily began running deeper into the forest, like she was a hound that had caught the scent of the fox. "Come on! I just found it!"

"Found what?" I jogged after her, hurdling the same fallen log she'd hurdled, but a few seconds later. "Why are you running so fast?"

"Puh-lease, you can keep up. You're the picture of fitness and strength, you beefcake farmer."

Beefcake! What did that mean? *It means Emily finds me hot.* My face and neck grew warm. I chased after her, but I'd lost her in the trees.

"Hey. Where did you go?" I couldn't see her anywhere. She'd entered one of those time vortices—as if this was crystal-connected Sedona instead of Maplebrook. "Emily?"

"Up here!" A hand shot down through the leaves and waved me upward. "It's perfect!"

She took my hand and pulled me upward, and I scrambled up the trunk and onto a branch beside the one where she sat—trusting it wouldn't give out under my weight. I mean, I had to weigh twice what she did, or more.

"See?" she asked, her face bright but dappled with sun and shade. "Can't you just picture it? The tree house! These branches all splay out like spokes on a wheel and at the same level. They're strong, symmetrical, and it's going to be amazing!"

"How did you notice it from so far away?" We'd run a fair bit. "And …" My throat caught. What was that? I reached toward it, and there was a short length of board nailed to a branch on the far side of Emily's *wheel.* "Sorry. Just a second."

I crawled toward the two-foot-long pine two-by-four with the huge nail down its center. It couldn't be! But it was. "You're not the first person to notice this tree's potential."

This was exactly the same tree. The very place where Dad had shown Neil and me his childhood tree house construction—stopped prematurely before anything could be termed a *house,* but still in evidence. We'd made big plans to continue building it, but then Dad had gotten caught up in Neil's model rocket, so I built one, too. We'd launched them near the stream.

"What is this?" Emily was at my side, on the same branch, but the weight didn't seem to even register for this venerable giant. "Someone else tried to build here, eh? See? Great minds think alike." She moved over to the next *spoke* and leaned back, stretching herself lengthwise on the branch beside mine, closing her eyes. "City girls don't get tree houses or covered bridges or things like that."

"But they want them?"

"Uh-huh." She peeked open one eye at me. "They do."

And did they want country guys, too? I didn't ask.

"Let's build it?" she said.

"One construction project at a time, Flash."

"Of *course* I mean we'd do this only if there's time." She sat up straight and pointed skyward. "Look! A few leaves at the top are turning golden. And there are some orange ones up there, too! Is it time yet?"

"Not usually, but …" But Yves had said the almanac predicted an unusual weather pattern. A freeze could turn the leaves, but usually the length of the day dictated it. "I guess we'll see, huh? So, are you ever going to tell me what made you buy the bridge?"

"Maybe. I can tell you this, though." She hopped down and we picked our way through the drying grass and over the fallen log, heading back toward the houses. "I said it was a childhood dream, but I wasn't totally a child. I was more like a teenager."

Ah. So, she was a romantic at heart. "I take it you've heard the alternate name for a covered bridge." I stifled a chuckle and tried to picture Emily as a swooning teen.

We crossed the orchard, weaving in and out among the tree trunks.

"What name?" she asked.

Had the girl heard nothing? First, no astronaut details, and now this? "The other name for a covered bridge is a *kissing bridge*. The lore was that they were originally footbridges and just long enough to secretly steal a kiss with a sweetheart as you crossed, and no one in town would be the wiser."

Emily's fair cheeks blossomed scarlet. "Honestly, I've never heard that term."

"You're sure?" Because it seemed like she was fibbing.

"Cross my heart." Her index finger drew an X over her heart. Yeah, I watched. "But—okay. I will admit that there was something to do with a kiss and a bridge that did capture my girlish heart."

"Not necessarily a covered bridge?" I left her side when a towering maple split us apart while we passed.

"Not initially, no. Originally I was fixated on suspension bridges. Brooklyn, Golden Gate. The big cables and arches fascinated me. They seemed romantic."

"Okay."

"Later, covered bridges caught my fascination. They're more

intimate. Quieter."

True. The one over the Maple Brook didn't even carry traffic. "You just got lucky when a covered bridge came up for sale?"

"Exactly!" She smiled. "It's the weirdest thing, but I don't think I'll ever regret it—even though my coworker Brenda called me a nut when I told her about it."

"She used the word *nut*?"

"Yep. Nut."

"Well, according to everyone in Maplebrook, you're not half the nut the other person who wanted to buy it was."

"I met Coolidge and his mustache."

"Then you've had the pleasure."

"Not my definition of pleasure." She climbed over the split-rail fence that demarcated the edge of the orchard and waited for me to follow. "Does he always threaten people when he's upset? Is that normal behavior for him?"

"He threatened you? With physical harm?" We ventured into the pasture.

"No, just that he'd get the bridge. Said I had *another think coming.*"

Oh. His vocal crutch. "Not sure how he treats everyone. To be honest, I kind of keep my distance, but Amos uses the word *hubris* to describe Coolidge."

"Foolish pride? I can see that."

What I didn't tell her was the rest of Amos's rant—the part about Coolidge's dream of trying to fix up bridges and ruining them in the process. For one, I didn't know whether that was even true, and for another, I didn't like saying negative stuff about people even if it was true.

We crossed the pasture, passed my spent vegetable garden behind the house, and came to the bridge. I needed to go across and do some more framing for the bedroom we were installing. Emily could have stayed at the farmhouse, but she kept walking alongside me.

We set foot on the bridge, side by side. Emily's shoulder bumped into my forearm. I was quite a bit taller than Emily. I was quite a bit taller than most. We didn't speak as we crossed. Was she thinking the same thing as I was? This could be a private walk, away from noticing eyes, a perfectly good place to steal a kiss?

It was always hard for me to guess what she was thinking. There was more that Emily France wasn't telling me.

Chapter 9

Emily

Kissing bridge! Who knew?

I lay in my bed a few nights later replaying one of my many, many conversations with Buzz. Buzz always possessed the best tidbits of information. He was a wealth of knowledge—all on topics I'd never studied.

I turned on my side, parting the curtains in the bedroom window, and looked across the property to where the bridge spanned the river.

My bridge.

My kissing bridge.

On the far side of it, lights were on in my under-construction house. Buzz must be burning the midnight oil. He'd sent me home at sundown, but now—there he was, still working. Either he was anxious to finish and swap houses back, or else he was just that kind to me.

Part of me feared it was the latter.

Another part hoped it.

No matter how nice he made Bridge Cottage though, I wouldn't be living in it long. Either I'd go back to work in Boston in a much-improved environment, swept clean of corrupt dealmakers, or I'd be sitting in jail beside them with cold showers, bread and water, and with a toilet in my cell—far worse than any outhouse.

Either way, the house would just be mine for the winter or until the trial date came. I hadn't checked online even once since coming to Maplebrook, so I was kept blessedly in the dark on any details that were unfolding in the investigation or the court case. The only person alive who had my number was Jerry, so I may as well have dropped off the face of the earth.

Sorry, Mom and Dad. We weren't in touch often, anyway. They wouldn't worry until Christmas. Unless they saw the news about Pokoa Financial.

Mom had taken Dad back after he finished serving his time. After that choice, I'd kept my distance—especially after they moved to Central America to rebuild their lives.

I closed the curtain and replayed my walk with Buzz across the bridge tonight—our skin grazing against each other's. I might have died of electrocution! It was all I could do to breathe during the whole crossing!

Yeah, even if I moved back to Boston, I wasn't going to be able to sell the covered bridge—at least not until I'd had one kiss on it.

After that, maybe I could loosen up. Sell it to that threatening fellow, since he wanted it so much. Where had I put his card, anyway? I'd grabbed it when I cleaned out the Mercedes when I sold it. That might turn out to be a good thing—for both of us someday.

I'd get my kiss, and he'd get his bridge.

Win-win.

And after the kiss—a very good kiss that I can feel all the way to my toes—he will drop to one knee, open up a ring box, and a diamond will glint its reflection in his hazel eyes.

Hazel! Who did I know with hazel eyes? Not Justin.

Buzz Atchison.

Oh, brother. I was not going to go down that road. He was too good—and too much married to his orchard. A confirmed bachelor, less likely than Amos to find a wife. He'd said so himself.

No way was I going to let myself get caught up in that fantasy.

***

Amos drove the rugged, two-seater open farm vehicle, with me in the passenger seat, gripping the bar for dear life. The guy didn't slow this side-by-side down for anything, foot fully depressed on the gas from the minute he took the wheel.

"Fall's a-coming," he shouted at me, taking his eyes off the orchard. "Then winter."

"And sugar maple sap."

"Yep, but not soon enough for Buzz."

"What do you mean?" I asked.

Amos looked at the road ahead—which wasn't a road—and jerked the wheel to keep from hitting a tree trunk squarely in our path. "Sap isn't until February at the earliest."

"And?" Buzz had told me that himself. It wasn't a trade secret. "And that's a problem because …?"

"Mortgage."

The M-word. "What about it? Doesn't it come due monthly?" I didn't know much about farm loans, but I did know loans, and nearly every one I'd ever heard of required monthly installments.

"Buzz's got himself a balloon. It's gonna pop if something big doesn't happen."

Balloon. I pressed my hand to my cheek, dragging it downward. "Balloon payment?"

"That's what I said." Amos dodged to miss a skunk trundling past us. If it sprayed, we were well out of spray distance by that time, such was our speed. "Buh-loon. He's the loon, if you ask me."

Loons got caught in those tricky mortgage schemes, for sure. "He must have had a good reason."

"Yup. He had to have the farm to pay for his great-aunt Fern's nursing home bill."

I didn't follow, but we angled down a steep slope, and I had to swallow a scream. I'd do better asking Buzz directly. Amos might be getting things mixed up.

But I didn't think he was as off about this as it might seem.

Amos dropped me off where Buzz stood beneath a sugar maple with a pole saw. The muscles in his back flexed as he sawed away at the dead branches, and more of them lay around his feet.

"Buzz? What's this about a balloon payment?" I shouted.

Buzz cut power to the blade. "Amos spilled the beans, huh? What all did he tell you?"

"It was confusing." I related to him the part that I'd understood. "I know it's not my business. But I'd like you to tell me anyway."

It took a while of Buzz mashing his lips together and pacing here and there, but finally, he cracked. "Last day of the year, and I owe nearly half the entire amount next year's harvest will bring in."

Half a year's profits! In a single day? "You don't have it?"

He shook his head. "This year wasn't stellar. The freeze ended too soon, and the trees budded. Sap stops flowing when the trees bud."

This was bad. Really bad. "Do you have a plan?"

"I'm working on one." He frowned, and that cloud I'd seen on his face the first day I met him came back—briefly. "Something will work out." He affected a sunny countenance.

It'd better work out. He couldn't lose Maplebrook Farm if he'd bought it out of family loyalty.

I'll start thinking. I'm great at thinking up business solutions. It might be the only thing I'm great at, but I should use my skills for him, after all he's doing for me.

Problem was, I knew nothing about the orchard business or how to expand it or to speed income. I refused to entertain the obvious idea of selling any portion of it.

"Now, Emily, it's only fair." Buzz took a step closer to me. I could almost feel his breath on my cheek. It smelled like apples.

"What is?" I squeaked. I cleared my throat. "What's only fair?"

"I told you the thing that's bothering me most." He looked earnest, like he actually wanted to know me better. Like he cared. "It's only fair if you share something, too."

An anvil landed in my stomach. I stepped back. "That wasn't the deal." I always knew the details of a contract before I signed. "Sorry."

Buzz's beautiful face fell, and I couldn't disappoint him. Not after all he'd done to bring me into his life.

Fine. I grabbed the imaginary contract and signed.

"What do you want to know?" The anvil hulked lower. "I'm an open book." *Lie, lie, lie.* I hated lies. I shoved them from my heart and mind.

"You're Emily England, not Emily France. Why the nom de plume or whatever?"

"How did you ...?" It didn't matter how he'd learned my name. While the lies were on banishment status, truth serum took over. If I was going to demand honesty from others, I should at least be honest. *I can trust Buzz,* my inner voice whispered. *He cares about honesty. He's been a hundred percent honest with me so far. Me, a stranger.*

No! I shushed the insistent voice, but then, all my ice walls crumbled, and I told him the truth about my situation. "I'm in Maplebrook"—my voice cracked—"because I'm hiding."

Slowly, Buzz nodded his head. "Well, then a couple of things make more sense."

"Like what?"

"Like the sudden disappearance of your *slick* car."

He'd noticed and connected it? "Like I said, it'd be conspicuous in Maplebrook."

"And your lack of need of a post office box."

Oh, he'd seen that, too. "I'm not great at flying under the radar, I guess."

"Nobody else would notice it, I bet. Well, Van and Greta, but they're too swamped with their store to do much digging into people's personal lives."

I exhaled and crumpled, flumping down onto an old and silvered semi-flat stump. "So, how did you figure out my last name?"

"Saw your driver's license and credit card."

True, I'd left my wallet flopped open a time or two during our trips to town, though I'd always paid for everything with the cash from my cleaned-out accounts. "Don't judge me by the photograph."

"Go ahead, tell me the rest, then."

"The rest?" I knew what he was getting at. I rubbed my nose and ear, which suddenly itched like I'd been attacked by a colony of mosquitoes. "Of what?"

"Of why you're hiding." His voice grew low, and he sat down on a clump of dry grasses beside me. "So I can protect you from whomever it is."

Normally, I'm Fort Knox when it comes to work confidentiality, but in this case, with Buzz Atchison offering to protect me, I couldn't help but let a few gold bars escape.

"The people I worked with in Boston turned out to be untrustworthy. They may have implicated me in a crime."

"Thus the questions about integrity."

"Exactly."

"So, what are you planning to do about it?" He went right for the jugular.

"Though it killed me to do so"—and it had more than killed my love for Justin—"I did the only thing I could do to preserve my integrity."

"You blew the whistle."

Exactly. Buzz's understanding had made that leap to the assessment of my character instantly. I exhaled just a little.

Maybe there remained one honest man in the world—and he was gazing at me from his spot on the yellowing grass with those warm hazel eyes that were saying so much to me right now.

He opened his mouth to speak, and I braced myself for him to offer pity, or worse, advice.

Instead, all he said was, "There's a harvest dance next Friday on your bridge. Go with me as my date?"

Chapter 10

Buzz

Friday came, and my head was still helium-filled. *She said yes. We have a date planned.*

It couldn't be real.

But it was.

We stood in my farmhouse's kitchen.

"For real, no one let you know that the annual harvest dance is always held on your covered bridge?" I asked Emily and picked at the remaining chicken bones on my plate from the rotisserie we'd shared.

"I guess everyone assumes I know the local traditions." Emily dumped her bones into the trash and placed the plate in the dishwasher. She took mine next. "That, or they don't realize who owns it. Though, I thought word had gotten around that I was the buyer."

Oh, it'd gotten around, all right. Coolidge the Colossal Clod had made sure of that. "Do you have a problem with letting the town use it for the harvest dance?"

"I think a bridge dance sounds fun. I haven't gone dancing since ... middle school?"

Unbelievable. The woman should be danced with, and often, and with someone who knew how. "It's great of you to just roll with it,

58

then, and not tell the village they can't use it."

She shut the dishwasher, and headed to the bedroom. "See you in a few."

"Where are you going?" I'd expected us to head down the slope of the yard toward the bridge. The music was already rattling the farmhouse's windows.

"To change my clothes. You said this is a dance, right?"

But it was a harvest dance, and she was already wearing jeans and a flannel shirt—basically a harvest dance official uniform. "You look nice as you are." Really nice. So nice I'd been thinking off and on about the covered bridge kiss all through dinner.

If we're dating, I can kiss her.

"Well, this is a date, right? I want to look good for a date."

Her back turned, and I made a fist-of-triumph. "Yep, it's a date." My first date since coming to Maplebrook, but she didn't need to know that. A few of the moms in the town had done their best to convince me to date their daughters, but up to now, I just hadn't felt like it.

From the moment I first saw Emily England, I'd felt like it. And I was feeling more and more like it every passing day. Every time we crossed the bridge together, she stayed as near to my side as if we were conjoined twins.

Ever since our conversation in the woods, when she'd opened up about the fact she was using Maplebrook as a sort of witness protection location, I'd been feeling so close to her, as if we were confidants. Friends who knew each other's secrets. At least she knew some of mine. Could I share the rest with her, like how I'd lost my hearing?

"Can you just—?" She appeared at my bedroom door, wearing a green velvet form-fitting dress that ended halfway down her thighs. The neckline was exactly what I would have asked for if Santa had let me make a wish list. She turned her back toward me and lifted her hair. The top of a zipper was slightly down.

Stars above, did she want me to raise or lower it?

I crossed the room in three strides and moved the zipper—realizing

59

in time what she was asking before I made a fool of myself. "There," I said, moving her hand, my fingers grazing the back of her neck and rearranging her hair. "All zipped."

My conversational skills took a trip to Tahiti. I'd just touched the softest skin I'd ever felt. Me, with my callused hands. My breaths were tight.

"Do I look okay for a harvest dance?" She turned around, and it was like one of those moments in a teen prom movie, when the heroine appears at the top of the stairs, and the hero—her date—waits at the bottom looking at her like his best dream has just come to life.

Pretty sure my face glazed over just like all those movie kids' had.

"What's wrong? Did I choose the wrong thing to wear?" She glanced down at her perfection. "I might break an ankle in these pumps, but no other shoes I brought with me would go with the dress."

"I'll—I'll carry you down to the bridge," the bullfrog living at the back of my throat croaked—just as if he were in love. "Hang on 'round my neck."

I scooped her up, with her legs dangling over my left arm, her body snugly secured to my chest.

"Buzz!" A giggle I'd never heard from her burst forth. "But I'm heavy."

Beg to differ—since I was made of helium and she was made of feathers. I floated us out the farmhouse door, down the porch steps, and over the grass toward the river. "You all right?" I asked as we descended the moonlit rock-strewn footpath toward the bridge. "You're not uncomfortable?"

Our eyes met, and she was staring at me, her pupils almost broad enough to eclipse her pale green irises. Slowly, she shook her head. She moistened her lips and I felt her arms go a little tighter around my neck. "I'm … fine."

Yes, indeed, she was fine. The finest woman I'd ever seen—and by far the finest woman I'd ever held in my arms. The only one I'd ever held in this fashion for sure— carry-across-the-threshold hold, if I'd had to describe it. My heart thrummed, and not from the exertion.

We were still a few strides from the light's spillage from the bridge, and I hesitated to step into it. Here, in the light of the full late-September moon, we were the only two people alive. The others' voices and the fiddle music faded to nothing. I paused, still holding her.

"You smell like apples," she whispered.

"You smell like heaven." The woman smelled like heaven. Truthfully, if I eventually got to heaven and it didn't end up scented like Emily, I'd ask for a transfer—it was that good. She always smelled like heaven. Mixed with cotton candy. "Sweet."

Her chin tilted upward, and I pulled her ever-so-slightly closer to me. Only a breath separated our lips. Hers parted, and—

"Buzz!" Amos's voice shattered the moment. "What-chew got in your arms? The mannequin from The Furniture Store? Oh, excuse me, Miss France."

She could have been Miss France—as in, on her way to the Miss Universe pageant—she looked that good. Ten, ten, ten, in all the competitions.

"Set me down, I guess," Emily whispered. "We're conspicuous."

I lowered her to the ground, my blood still coursing like it was competing in the historic Mille Miglia Italian road race. "Are you ready to go dance?"

"I love dancing." Her ankle wobbled. "Just kidding. I'm not a great dancer."

"I am. Follow me." I'd been at enough of these harvest dance events to realize the requirement in the spring—after the syrup-making finished—was to take a swing class. I'd done four rounds of classes now and wasn't too bad, if I could brag a little. "It's not hard."

"You can dance?" Her eyes were wide.

"I'm no Fred Astaire, or that guy on *Strictly Ballroom*, but I can—"

He dragging gasp shut down my excuse. "You know the movie *Strictly Ballroom*? Is it crazy that I don't dance, but that that is my

61

favorite movie of all time?" A smile spread across her face, showing her pretty, white teeth for the first time tonight. "You, my date, are a million surprises."

"I'm not that interesting," said the guy who'd lived in Neil's shadow for thirteen years. But—no. I was with Emily. And she liked *me*. The farmer side, the boring engineer side, the make-do amateur carpenter. And she might even like my dancing.

We weaved our way through a crowd of locals as I led her by the hand to the center of the bridge. The din of their conversation combined with the music for a festive noise. Laughs punctuated the air. A guy from the gas station pointed finger guns at me and fake-shot, adding a wink and a tongue-click.

Okay, yeah, I did have the prettiest date in the world.

The pastor's wife raised wiggling brows, elbowed her husband, and he gave me an approving nod. I was officially on display with Emily England. A few local mothers frowned.

Nothing I could do about that.

The center of the bridge was less packed than the edges where the glazed doughnuts and fragrant spiced apple cider were being served. It was time to dance.

"Just step toward me, and then pull apart. Keep your arms a little tense, but loosen the rest of you. Hold to my fingers like this." Her hands were in mine. She was stepping toward me, pulling away, and then we were together again. Just the simplest of starting moves.

"Now, I'm going to let go with one hand and you'll roll out, and then I'll roll you back in. Like this." We did it, easy as pie, and we were dancing with her back to me, in a hug. Instead of continuing the swing just now, I opted to sway, to hug her closer, to bury my nose at the spot just behind her ear. We swayed back and forth, with me breathing her intoxicating scent and thinking about how to keep this fragrance, this feeling in my life.

Eventually, we did the swing some more.

Two hours later, the DJ announced the last song, and I held Emily in my arms for the final slow dance. Even though it ended, I kept her in my arms, turning in a slow circle at the center of the bridge's makeshift dance floor as the organizers took down the party decorations.

Normally, I'd help carry sound equipment to trucks or fold up tables, but tonight, I held Emily instead.

Someone swept the bridge's floor near us. The lights went off as someone hauled them away, too. Everyone else left. We stayed on the bridge alone, swaying.

"Don't ever downplay your dance skills." I held her close. "You're a natural."

"You make me feel like a natural woman." She quoted that old song and then followed up her cheesy comment with that giggle that penetrated my every cell. "Sorry. I quote lyrics when I get nervous."

"I don't make you nervous."

"You, Buzz Atchison, make me nervous."

"That's so hard to believe."

"Why? You're exactly the type of man to make a woman like me very nervous."

"In what universe am I that guy?"

"Do I have to spell it out?" When I didn't reply but kept swaying, she finally spelled it out. "You're pretty much everything an ideal guy should be—capable, strong, innovative, fearless, handsome. Honest."

Who was she describing? Not me.

Emily loosed herself from my grasp and looked right at me. Her eyes searched mine, with her eyebrows pushed together. "What is it?"

"What's what?"

"Come with me." She took me by the hand and led me to the west end of the bridge, the side with her tumble-down dwelling where I lived. We stood under the moonlight instead of in the dark at the center of the bridge where I'd been dreaming of kissing her a minute ago. Her face was pretty as always, but right now it was stern. An important conversation loomed—I just never wanted to have it.

"Now, talk to me."

"What do you mean?"

"You, my date, can't take a compliment. Since the first day we met, I've suspected you have a story to tell—a story a lot bigger than a balloon payment on a mortgage."

The ground quaked beneath me. Or maybe it was just me. "Um."

"Buzz. Please. You can tell me."

I—maybe I could. I swallowed hard. "It's not flattering. And I would assume you should know it by now. It's the top result when you put my name into any internet search engine."

"I am offline, off the grid."

Oh, right. In hiding.

I stood petrified, a ten million-year-old hunk of redwood.

"Buzz. Don't *make* me go online. Tell me. In your own words. Reporters always get things wrong. They mishear things or put their own spin on a story. It's disgusting. I want you to tell me what happened to you. It has something to do with your brother."

The air grew still—or maybe I lost what remained of my hearing, because everything was muffled. My tongue got fuzzy as my face heated.

She wanted to hear it from my point-of-view. No one ever asked for that.

I cleared my throat, but the words still didn't come.

Looking up at me, Emily softened. Then, she sank against me, laying her head on my chest, reaching her arms to link around my waist.

So, instead of giving me a stare down, like I might have expected of someone as direct as she was, she pressed her ear to my heart, as if my heart could tell the story in Morse code, and she was listening to decipher its deepest resonance.

I held her that way for a while, my tightness unspooling.

After a few moments, she lifted her hand, pointing to a bright star near the western horizon. "That's Venus. She hasn't set yet. And if you look to the east, that's Jupiter—with Saturn just a little ahead in the rotation."

"You know your planets."

"They're usually the only *stars* I can see in the city."

That's true. Cities' lights obscured the sky's majesty. I'd hated that when I lived and worked in Concord. Some even called it light pollution, and I couldn't disagree.

The planets shone so brilliant and predictable above us, and the ground beneath me quit quaking. I felt connected to the past, present, and future at once, and I could speak at last.

"One time, I took a fall climbing alone and lay in the snow for two nights after my accident. I was at Fort Lewis. I'll never forget how the constellations moved slowly across the sky."

"Fort Lewis. That's in eastern Washington."

"Yeah. It's where the US Air Force survival school is." And where my Air Force career ended. "I gauged the progress of Orion from east to west, all night long. It gave me an idea of how long it would be before the sun came back." Long, painful hours. "It's the coldest I've ever been."

"Winter?" she asked. "You were out two nights in the cold?"

"Yeah, I would have just gone back, but my left femur had snapped, as well as my right tibia. For the first while, I was determined to get myself back to the top. I tried climbing the ropes that still dangled, but without the use of my legs for counterbalance, I couldn't make progress. I even crawled on my elbows as far as I could, but I was at the bottom of a ravine."

"Buzz." Emily said my name like a prayer. "You survived that? You're ... wow. That's so brave."

That was a new twist on it. Usually everyone ... well, I'd see how Emily reacted after I told her the rest. "It was a required course for Air Force officers to complete. I had the goal to be an officer, a pilot. My brother, too. We were in the officer training courses, tracking for NASA's notice. We had the right education, the right experience." Both of us, up until that moment. "It worked out for him."

"That's nice, but what about your legs? How can you walk so

65

normally? Why didn't you freeze to death?" She nestled closer to me. "How are you here?"

Again, she ignored my references to Neil and only seemed interested in me. Would that last when I told her the rest? "I have my brother to thank. It's supposed to be a solo experience, but Neil claimed he had some kind of *twin ESP* and felt an urgency that he needed to seek me out, that I was in trouble. He left his solitary camp, scoured the area for thirty-six hours, and found me at the bottom of the valley. I heard him calling for me, and I called back. He rappelled down, lashed me to his back, and then in a feat of sheer adrenaline, packed both of us out."

"Buzz." Emily didn't comment on Neil's heroism—a first in my experience. "I'm so thankful you held on."

"To Neil?"

"To life."

Tears sprang to my eyes. I didn't know what was happening, but they fell uncontrollably. They shot down my face like they were jet-propelled. I swiped them away, over and over, thanking sweet mercy that Emily gazed at Jupiter and Saturn and not at me.

They subsided as quickly as they'd appeared. "Thanks," I managed. "Me, too." Or else I might not have this moment, with this woman, under those same stars.

"Now I understand you a little more." At last, she looked up at me in the moonlight. "You don't walk with any limp. It's amazing."

"The military doctors treated me with kid gloves. I got the best care, especially while the story made the news circuit." I'd tell her about Neil's parades of fame some other time. "There was just one thing they couldn't repair."

"Oh?"

"You've probably noticed I ask you to repeat things now and then."

"Sure. I just figured you're like about a fourth of the people in my life who suffer from hearing loss."

"I'm not the only person you know who can't hear?"

"Of course not." Her shoulder, pressing into my chest, rose and fell slightly. "How did the accident cause it?"

"Frostbite. It crept from my outer ear to my inner ear, where it settled and harmed my hearing." It took a steadying breath to say the rest. "My legs healed perfectly. I thought I was going to get right back onto the pre-NASA track. I was one semester away from my aeronautical engineering degree. I'd continued my officer training classes, I'd stayed up with everything, and I was ready to get back at it."

"But the hearing loss"—she heaved a sigh for me—"changed your path."

"You could say that." Destroyed my path, more like. Detonated it with an IED. "They thought my hearing would recover. When it didn't …"

She rested her head against my chest. Her heartbeat timed with mine. I held her, but she held me more. In that moment, someone at last sorrowed with me over the losses I'd endured.

I should have been able to bury them all before now, but it helps to have someone else mourn.

"Have you ever considered that maybe the changes put you on a nobler path?"

Nobler? Than being a pioneer in space? Ha. "More important than my parents' aspirations for me and the goals I'd set for myself?"

"I don't know. I mean, without that alteration of your trajectory, would you have had the chance to rescue the orchard and keep it in the family?"

Huh? I paused to think.

"Probably not." Actually, that was a hard no. I would have been too busy running experiments, piloting a rocket, experiencing low-earth orbit to care about a family orchard.

"Because of that loss, you did gain something—I think. Something bigger."

Bigger than space? The orchard was big, but … "The results of scientific experiments performed in space contribute to advancements in agriculture, biomedicine, technology in general. It's a good field. It's worthwhile."

"Of course it is." She slipped her hand down my arm and threaded her fingers between mine, but she didn't say anything else. She had more to tell me, I could feel it vibrating in her.

"What aren't you saying, Emily?"

She looked up at me. "Answer me this: who could perform those experiments?"

"Any of the men who were elite enough to be accepted into the program and continue in it to fulfill the missions." Neil, for instance.

"In other words, a number of men or women at NASA or in the military."

"So?"

"Don't take this wrong. There's probably a gentler way to put this, but you seem as straightforward as I am. At NASA, you were replaceable."

"A hundred percent." This was not making me feel better. They'd replaced me in the program within moments. I'd even been replaceable in my engineering firm. Someone else could fill my spot.

"Buzz, when it came to saving Maplebrook Farm and keeping it in your family, you were not replaceable."

"Well ..." Wasn't I, though?

"Think about it. No one else could have, or would have, taken on the task."

I stilled. Emily's words settled over me like a silken blanket. She was right—no one else could or would have rescued Maplebrook Farm from being sold to either a new orchard owner or, worse, an investor who wanted to sell its age-old forest for the sawmill.

I am irreplaceable in the position where I am right now. Other paths had been yanked out of my life so that I could tread this very road—a road only I could walk.

My mind expanded three sizes.

"From what I've heard, by buying the orchard you made it so your great aunt could continue receiving health care as well. You were a blessing to many generations."

"How do you know that?" I'd never told Emily. "Let me guess. Amos."

"Amos," she confirmed.

Good old Amos. "Great-Aunt Fern passed away two years after I bought Maplebrook Farm." And even though I hadn't ever told people about it, as it wasn't something I could take credit for, the farm's purchase had financed her care. "She loved this place. My dad, too."

Okay, fine. But there was a big caveat here. If I could keep it afloat, yeah—I'd be irreplaceable. But only if I could keep it out of hock.

"Look at what you've done for your family, Buzz. You're a hero."

Was I? If I was in her eyes, then … my chest expanded, my spine straightened, the sky's stars sharpened into focus. There were six sextillion stars—and I could see all of them, in Emily's eyes. "Emily?"

"Yes, Buzz?" She lifted her chin, her face turned toward me at last.

I lifted her up and onto the ledge of the bridge's lattice. Sitting on it, she was my height, making us face to face, eye to eye. *Soon lip to lip?* I moved her arms, setting her hands on my shoulders. I placed my hands on her hips.

"Emily, you're the most insightful woman I've ever met." Her perfume filled my senses again, and her eyes were large in the moonlight. "I probably don't even need to mention you're also the most beautiful."

Here on the kissing bridge, I ached to kiss this woman who made me feel connected to life, to family, to history, to myself. *To her.*

Then, to my shock and awe, Emily leaned closer to me, placing a soft kiss on my jaw.

All the stars fell in brilliant, meteoric flame as her lips grazed my skin. I burst into flames and let out a groan as she placed another kiss near my ear.

"I'm afraid you'll have to repeat yourself," I said.

"If you insist," she said. Her kisses trailed downward to the side of my neck, where sensations radiated best. How could she know that about me? She was a psychic, or she was crazy intuitive about me—body and soul.

I closed my eyes and groaned as she kissed that spot, and then others, and then worked her way up toward my cheek, my temple. She pressed herself more tightly against my torso, and then—I could hold back no longer, and I took her into my arms, taking her lips like they belonged to me. She returned the kiss with a sigh of pleasure.

"Buzz, mmm." She allowed me to drink her in. And I drank deeply, as a man who has been on a desert island who finally finds fresh water. Emily was my oasis. My respite, my refreshment. My soul swam in a rising tide of longing that might never subside.

Chapter 11

Emily

Kissing Buzz Atchison not only on the covered bridge but also under the stars was a revelation even more than it was a wish fulfilled. I clung to him like he was the only light left in a darkening world. Our mouths moved in a rhythm that drove my pulse into a jungle beat. I couldn't stop kissing him. I needed him. We were the kiss, and the kiss was life and meaning and truth and the universe.

He pulled me closer, and I dissolved into a rush of helplessness against the rising desire for his touch.

"Buzz," I managed, pulling away before anything went too far out to sea and pulled us under the waves. "I'm so glad I bought the covered bridge."

"Indeed." He scrubbed his hand down his cheek like he was coming-to after a long bout of unconsciousness.

Made sense—our kiss had been like living in a coma but with a single sensation: desire. The guy turned me to fire. It was like nothing I'd ever experienced before.

In the moonlight, his features were silver and gold. He was silver and gold. He had a drunken look on his face, love drunk. He pulled a lopsided, charming grin, one I'd seen once before, and it tickled the bottom of my stomach. "I'd much rather meet you on the bridge than old Coolidge," he said.

Wince. "Same here."

We interlinked our fingers, and Buzz helped me down from the railing. He walked me home—to his house—where he kissed me once more on the farmhouse porch. A chaste, brief kiss, but one that said he wasn't merely there for the one-time experience of bliss we'd ignited minutes ago.

Or had it been an hour? Time seemed so fleeting, so irrelevant, such a false construct.

I lay in my bed thinking of the kiss, replaying it—mmm—and glad for more days to come with Buzz Atchison as my neighbor and kissing friend. *And my boyfriend? Or more?*

***

Dating Buzz for the next few weeks consisted of more of our daily lives and work and meals together—but with a lot more kissing.

Because of a cold snap, fall had settled on Maplebrook like a tapestry of everything golden. Even the twilights of evening reflected gold at the sunsets' horizon. I'd never experienced nature so closely in the fall. As John Steinbeck said, my soul resonated to this landscape. *I wish I never had to leave Maplebrook.*

Kissing Buzz was incredible. I never wanted to stop that, either.

However, we did pause the make-outs to focus on our tasks of finishing the Bridge Cottage before the winter months set in. Fall was here in its glorious blaze of color, but those colors were warning flags that we needed to get a serious move on.

Work progressed on the shack, which was quickly becoming more habitable every day. We finished building the bedroom, framing it, adding wiring, drywall, lighting. We installed the bathroom plumbing and fixtures and a small cabinet. We added paint to the textured walls, and then the flooring went down, shipped in to Maplebrook by The Furniture Store.

"All that's left is to hang curtains and move in the furniture." I threw my arms around Buzz. "You did it!"

"You did it, too." True, but he'd done most of it. He kissed the top of my head.

We walked through, and then toured the outside. It had gone from dumpy to darling in such a short time. The interior's buttercup-yellow walls and bright white trim made it cheery, as did the eyelet curtains and vintage-turquoise appliances. Outside, we'd repaired all the siding, refreshed it with a coat of white paint, and hung cute hunter-green shutters, and added some shrubbery. Next spring, the flower boxes would spill over with geraniums or petunias.

Darling for sure.

"Not bad. It's even toasty warm in here—especially compared to outside." Frost painted the windowpanes with flowers and feathers, but the pot-belly stove kept the rooms warm and comfortable.

"The cold came early this fall." He frowned, looking outside like it was his enemy instead of autumn in New England, a dream travel destination for half the world. "I shouldn't be surprised to get a hard freeze or two in October, but we've had two straight weeks of it."

Something was off with him all of a sudden, but I didn't want to spoil the moment by asking more now. Instead, I asked, "Will it snow? This place would be incredibly beautiful with snow. And with nothing to do until sap time in the late winter—I can picture a lot of cozy time with my handsome neighbor between now and then."

He took me in his arms. "I do like that." He kissed me a while near the fire, and lots of things got warm.

Soon enough, I needed to pull back or things would go from warm to hot, so I said, "I'll make dinner in my new kitchen and we can eat it here to celebrate."

"Sounds great. I've got something to check out first, but I'll be back." Buzz left, and I got busy cooking.

I'd bought a few choice ingredients that matched my recipe when I was at The Furniture Store, and luckily they'd had fresh tarragon. When it warmed up enough to eat outside again, I could make this meal and have it waiting in the tree house we would build.

Am I staying here next summer? The thought troubled and excited me at once. In a way, now that I'd lived like this, it was hard to picture going back to my life in the world of high finance, with its incessant pressures and wide swath of effects on people's lives.

Maplebrook was feeling like home, even though it'd only been a couple of months. I could live in the Bridge Cottage and ... do what? I didn't know. So, I kept making dinner in my new kitchen while Buzz stayed out on his errand. Every minute he was gone, I felt his absence.

Did that mean something? *I can't be in love yet. But I might be getting there.*

An hour later, the tarragon chicken was finished, and Buzz still hadn't come back. I set the table for two, lit a candle in the center and waited.

Finally, there was a sound in the yard. I went to the door, threw it open, which let the warm air out, but I didn't care because Buzz was here, and—no. It wasn't Buzz in the frost-covered yard.

"Rosie?" I hustled her inside. "It's cold out there. Let me get you something warm to drink." I brought her a mug of hot cider from the kettle. "To what do I owe this visit?" We hadn't planned on a housewarming party, but maybe we should—we could invite Amos, Van, Greta, Rosie, a few others. Celebrate the accomplishment.

"I just closed down the post office for the night, and I knew I had to come by. I'm not really sure how this letter found its way to me, but I thought it might be important enough to bring to you right away." From inside her parka she pulled a large manila envelope, thick, and with a heavy layer of tape over the clasp. "It had a law firm's name on it, so I didn't return it like I normally would."

Only Jerry knew I was here. "It's all right." I took the package from her and set it on the counter. "Thank you so much for making the trip. It's ridiculously cold out there."

"Coldest October on record. If it doesn't thaw a little, we're in for frozen pipes. Be sure to leave a trickle of water running tonight." She looked around the cottage, as if for the first time. "Is this even the same shack?" She stepped toward the stove and warmed her hands in front of it. "This stove, I remember. The rest is foreign. Good work. No wonder you've made so many trips to The Furniture Store."

Then, her eyes landed on the table setting with the lit candle and the two well-presented plates of dinner. "You're planning for company. Romantic company." Her eyes crinkled near the sides. "Do I guess correctly that you took my advice to *see well*."

"I did, Rosie. And you were right, once I looked, I could see very clearly."

She came over and gave me a hug. Then, she bundled back up. At the door, she paused and turned to me again. "I'm hoping that envelope only contains only good news, even though mail from a law firm rarely does. We all like having you around Maplebrook, but if you leave, there's one person I'm thinking won't recover."

She wasn't referring to her brother Amos. "Do you mean me?"

Rosie gave me a slightly sad smile, patted her heart, and left.

I ripped open the envelope. Page flip, page flip, page flip. Notes from findings, interviews, legal research. It was like looking at a foreign language I used to speak and which was coming back to me and morphing my brain back into condition. It took a second to reacclimatize to the terms and jargon that used to be my lifeblood.

The final page contained Jerry's analysis and recommendation for my future. Every word snipped a cord that connected me to the blimp that had held me aloft for the past couple of months. Soon, I was sinking—into a raging sea.

I stared through the curtains at the few visible brilliantly colored tree branches scraping at the gray sky. Brown and red, gold and still-green. The view shouted beautiful dissonance with my ugly feelings.

"Sorry that took so long." The cottage door banged open, and Buzz thundered in, peeling off his coat and gloves. "We had a frozen pipe near the sugar shack, and there was a leak I had to stop at the water main. Dinner smells amazing, and—are you all right?"

Buzz came and seated himself beside me on my nice couch we'd moved over from the farmhouse. He placed an arm around me, but he didn't peek at the paperwork.

I shoved it back in the envelope, my fingers and my voice trembling. "I'm afraid my past is catching up to me."

He pulled me closer, and I hugged him like letting go would drop me off a skyscraper.

"You're going?"

"Yes. No. I don't know." I hadn't digested everything in Jerry's final analysis, but I had definitely seen the dates of the depositions and the trial. "It looks like I have to go back to the city sooner than I'd expected."

"Will you stay the winter?"

Chapter 12

Buzz

I trudged back to the farmhouse after dinner—dinner I'd allowed to get cold by being distracted by the broken pipe.

I could have just shut off the valve and gone back to it later, after spending time with Emily. I could have been there for her in the moment that she'd received the Packet of Bad News which threatened to rip her away from Maplebrook and the home she'd built with me for her refuge from all those horrors.

But I'd chosen the orchard.

And she was being forced to choose the city.

Maybe we were too entrenched in our responsibilities for any of this to work. She was a city creature. Honestly, by spending all this time at the orchard, her career might have been squandered. She was clearly gifted in her career prior to coming to Maplebrook, or she wouldn't have driven that slick car or had cash to buy the covered bridge property.

I needed to know more about what terrible thing could have been in that envelope of doom to turn her pale and trembling. In all the weeks, now months, I'd known her, she'd never once gone pale or trembled. She was a rock.

Even though Emily hadn't researched me, which I truly appreciated, a few days after the envelope arrived she still hadn't recovered her good cheer. So, I broke down and ran a cursory internet search on her name, finding a handful of older articles at the top of the search bar.

Rising star in the finance world, Emily England takes the Ferr Corporation to the next level.

Emily England named MVP at Pokoa Financial for the fourth year in a row.

Looking for the next meteoric rise in the finance world? Keep your eyes on Emily England.

And then, a more recent article's headline caught my eye.

Pokoa Financial in ruins. Top adviser Emily England AWOL during investigation.

My throat dried out. I scanned the rest of the article. A lot of the financial terms were outside of an engineer-turned-orchard-farmer's jargon skill set, but one thing I knew: Emily's situation was dicey.

Kind of like my situation with the mortgage. We'd slogged through the calendar and were now another month closer to the due date of my balloon payment—and I still didn't have a solution. The freeze outside in nature felt like it might creep inside me once again and damage something else. Like my hope.

Especially if Emily left Maplebrook.

One thing I knew—I wasn't ready for her to leave. And I might never be. She'd become the golden threads in the fabric of my landscape's tapestry. I was accustomed to her being around. I loved eating meals with her, working alongside her, holding her. From the moment she came to Maplebrook, my loneliness fled.

I cleared my internet search and went outside to chop wood. Whack-crack. Whack-crack. The air smelled like wood fires, and the cold stung my cheeks and forehead.

Whack-crack, the logs split and fell to the ground beside the stump I used as a chopping block.

Here was the hinge-point question that plagued me: should Emily spend her life in Maplebrook anyway, even if this horrific meltdown of her current employer's company ended? She was a whiz kid, a notable figure on the landscape of big-time finance. If she hung out with slow-growing maple trees, she would be squandering her gifts, just like I'd instinctively known. I would be stealing her gifts from the world by selfishly keeping her here.

I couldn't ask her to do that. Not in good conscience. Not if I had any integrity—which seemed to be a sticking-point attribute for her. *And no wonder, if her company's integrity was in question as seriously as it seemed to be from those articles.*

Besides, who was I to think she didn't just see me as a pleasant pastime while she hid out? A failed Air Force officer, someone who needed to be rescued by a stronger brother from a fallen and broken place, someone who purchased an orchard with intent to save it but who could lose it anyway and have to start over in his mid-thirties?

What appeal could I have for a woman like Emily England?

A guy like Neil could win her.

A guy like me, though? Despite all the kind things she'd said to me the night we first kissed on the bridge, and the other times she'd built my ego, those were just words. I didn't match her description of me, not through-and-through.

"That's jest about close to enough wood to heat the whole town for a week." Amos rolled up on the ATV. "You working out your feelings since your Emily is probably leaving town?"

"You learn things by osmosis, Amos?"

"By reverse osmosis." He tapped his temple. "Means I asked my sister."

Rosie had brought the Packet of Bad News the other day, so she'd probably made some assumptions.

"Whether she's a-leaving or not, you gotta enjoy every second you got her and not mope like a dope. Will she want to stay if you're moping? Nope." He paused a minute and then broke into one of his fainter laughs. "See, I gots poetry in me today."

"You'll be the next Robert Frost," I lied. Although, he did have a point. Being morose wouldn't help my situation, and it wouldn't entice Emily to stick around—even if she ultimately couldn't.

If she could, though ... good for her. Better for me, but still—good for Emily. She does seem happy here, content, calm. I know it's good for her, compared to city life. I'm going to try to coax her to stay, or at least come back after the trial.

"What do you suggest, then, Amos?"

"Get her a real nice Christmas present."

"Like what?"

"I don't know. Take her shopping, see what she gets all giddy-faced over. Then buy it in secret." He grinned and patted himself on the chest with both gloved hands. "I could win me a woman if I wasn't a confirmed bachelor. See?"

"Maybe you should change your mind, Amos. Some woman would be lucky to get a thoughtful guy like you."

"Darn straight."

Amos roared off on the ATV, and I walked over to Bridge Cottage and knocked on the door. "Emily? You home? Let's go shopping."

She grabbed her coat and we rode into Maplebrook.

They'd fired up the furnace in The Furniture Store to summertime heat levels, and even though it was still early November, Van and Greta had already Christmased out, as Greta put it. "It's cold enough this week that the only thing to warm us is the thought of Christmas."

The place smelled like cinnamon and vanilla. We browsed the wrapping paper, the mega-boxes of Scotch tape, the candy aisle. We looked over locally handmade scarves, artist's sets, books with photography of New England's seasons. Emily didn't seem captured by anything in particular but acted like she liked it all.

This trip wasn't helping me accomplish anything.

"I've been thinking," she said as we passed the locally jarred maple syrup display. "Do they only collect sap in the spring? Can it

ever be collected in the fall?"

"Not this fall. It's too cold."

"Oh." She frowned. "Maybe it will suddenly warm up."

"Nope. We're in for the long haul of this iceberg weather, if past is prologue. Winters in Vermont are solid."

Van walked up and offered us a piece of homemade peanut brittle from a plate. "You'll like this. A touch of molasses. Greta put it in at my request."

It was good—and the molasses gave it depth. "Thanks."

He moved away, and Emily took my hand.

"Have you ever tasted maple sap straight from the tree? I wonder if you can just drink it without concentrating it."

"It's not as sweet."

"Is that a terrible thing? I mean, people drink coconut water. Isn't it similar?"

"Probably. Why?"

"Oh, just some ideas I was kicking around." She didn't expound on them. "Hey, look!" Emily pulled me toward a display of a Christmas tree decorated with little teddy bears. "I bet Greta strung her own popcorn for this." So it hadn't been the teddy bears to fascinate her. Unfortunate, since that'd be an easy gift, if not original.

In truth, I couldn't keep my peripheral attention off the jewelry case at the back of the store, filled with vintage necklaces, bracelets, and antique rings—including a diamond ring. Used, but it sparkled like it wanted out of the case and onto someone's finger.

Please! I couldn't just leap into buying Emily a ring for Christmas. We'd only been dating a month. We'd only known each other three months. I needed to let her go back to her life, but couldn't her life *also* be here? With me? The place she'd left seemed to give her nothing but scars. Being here healed her.

She fits in Maplebrook. She's at peace here. Plus, she's everything I need. Everything I want.

If I'd had even a few hundred bucks, I would have negotiated for that ring. Hung onto it, just in case. Maybe given it to her after inviting my parents up to meet her. Dad hadn't been here for years, and he might want to help tap the trees and collect sap once for old times' sake, before—

The bell jingled. In walked the official buzz-kill of the Holiday Pre-season: Yves. "Greta, I'll take a chicken salad on croissant sandwich. Oh, and a cruller, please."

I ducked behind the cowboy hat display. If he didn't see me, he wouldn't ask me in front of Emily if I was on track to make the payment.

"Sure thing, Yves." Greta wrapped the banker's order in white paper. "What's new?"

"The almanac calls for a major thaw."

Greta, whose face I could see, blinked at him a moment. "You read the almanac?"

"You sold it to me." Duh, his tone said. "Anyway, it's full of interesting details. And it's rarely wrong." He paid her and headed for the door, where he paused. "Good to see you, Buzz. I'll watch for you on New Year's Eve, right?"

Ugh.

"Who was that?" Emily brought over a box of popcorn. "Is there a New Year's Eve party I should know about? Are they going to use the bridge again?"

"There's a Christmas party first," Greta supplied the answer while my head spun with too many other thoughts. "You guys going to that together? Assert your continuing reign as Maplebrook's official cutest couple?"

"If nothing else, as the date of the most beautiful woman in Maplebrook," I said. Dancing with her again sounded great. I took the popcorn and paid for it. "You'll go, right?"

Emily nodded, reaching into the popcorn. "I'd love to."

"See you at the dance," Greta called. "The last big town event before New Year's Eve."

New Year's Eve hit me like a juggernaut. What would happen to Maplebrook Farm, and to me, on January first?

Chapter 13

Emily

The trial date loomed.

The last of the reds, golds, and browns of the leaves clung to the trees, until one night when the wind blew a fury, taking them all down, and leaving branches stark and bare.

Frostbitten villagers complained loudly about the cold when I eavesdropped in The Furniture Store.

"This cold is wrecking the pumpkin harvest," one said.

"And the tourism season," said another.

"Couldn't this cold weather potentially be a good thing for the syrup?" I asked, but all I got were dirty looks.

When I asked Buzz at dinner, he didn't completely shut me down. "Some say a very cold winter will make the sap sweeter, but not everyone agrees."

Buzz went to the orchard to work with Amos to remove branches that had fallen in that awful windstorm—and I seized my chance to get better information to confirm or deny my hunch about the sap.

Even though it was against my isolation protocol, I went over to the farmhouse and logged onto the internet, treading carefully—not going to any social media or email pages—just searching the maple syrup production sites and getting off.

Honestly, it felt weird going back to digital connection after so long away. Like putting on shackles after freedom.

Three sites, four. And then, yes! There it was! Exactly the information I'd suspected existed! I jotted down notes, a few phone numbers, a list of the websites where I'd found the best stuff. I folded the pages and tucked my notes deep into my coat. Exhilarated, I hustled toward the covered bridge. My covered bridge. My very own kissing bridge—literally.

I set foot on it, curbing my hurry—for this was sacred ground. Its dim shadows weren't remotely sinister. Rather, they held a romantic glow. Here, I'd first met Buzz. Here, he'd danced with me. Here, he'd kissed me back when I'd hinted at my growing love for him by being the first to show affection.

"Emily," a man's voice rolled through the air.

I'd been so caught up in my excitement about my findings about the maple sap that I hadn't seen the person poised on the other side of the bridge, his back against the railing, reclining like a cowboy with his back against a saloon wall.

"Coolidge?" I asked. "I've told you I'm not interested in—"

"Who's Coolidge?" The man stepped away from the side and into a shaft of light. "Don't you even recognize your boyfriend?"

The form took shape and registered for me. "Justin?" I stopped cold. "Clarification: ex-boyfriend." I backed up a couple of steps.

Justin advanced.

My nervous system kicked into *hunted* mode. I should bolt. I should make for my truck.

But it was on the other side of the covered bridge. I'd have to get around Justin to reach it.

"I found her!" he hollered. Instantly, he was flanked by another unmistakable silhouette: Pokoa's, round and squat.

"It's cold here, Emily." Justin came closer. "How can you stand it?" They stalked toward me, their prey, making me retreat a few more paces. "Nice bridge, though. So *this* is what you were rattling on about when you were trying to distract me from the fact you were gathering evidence against your own coworkers and sabotaging potentially the billion-dollar deal of a lifetime. It's sweet. Quaint. Very *you*." Menace laced Justin's voice.

I'd sent my phone to Jerry. There'd been no one to call for so long, I hadn't needed or wanted one. Besides, I'd been able to see Buzz nearly every waking moment, and he was the main person in my life here in Maplebrook.

But I'd been too clever by half. Because without a phone, I couldn't call for help.

I swallowed hard and mustered some fake confidence. "I'm glad you like the bridge." I didn't like, though, that Justin was there, defiling it. How could I have imagined for a moment that I'd ever want Justin to kiss or propose to me here?

My ears roared with an adrenaline rush. There were no houses near the brook but Buzz's and mine, and Buzz was on the other side of the orchard today. Never had I wished his orchard was a quarter-acre instead of a sprawling mountainside. Until now.

"I'm glad you bought the bridge. Brenda's the one who finally told us about it. Isn't it nice for you that you have a friend who really listens to you? Brenda just *soaks up* the details of your life. Even better, she's kind enough to share those details with those who care about where you are—when no one else can seem to find you."

Brenda. I closed my eyes for the briefest moment, but during that breath of inattention, Justin and Pokoa came closer. They were within a few feet now.

I feigned calm, channeling my skills honed from years of ice-cold business negotiations. "How is Brenda? How are you, actually? I didn't mean to hurt you with that text. It's not the most sensitive way to break up a year-long relationship. I realize that." If I turned around and ran, I could get to the far end of the bridge, I could disappear into the Maplebrook Farm orchard, climb into the tree house tree's branches and hide. They wouldn't find me. Snow hadn't fallen. They couldn't track my footprints.

"Yeah, Brenda's fine." Justin, too, could be ice-cold. "I got over the breakup pretty fast when I heard what you'd done. Forwarding an eyes-only email to the Securities and Exchange Commission?" He tsked three times. "Not a team-player move, Emily."

Mr. Pokoa cracked his knuckles.

"Are you here to threaten me, Justin? Or are you, Mr. Pokoa?"

"No, no, not at all." Justin obviously served as the sole spokesman for this shakedown. "We're here to negotiate. Quid pro quo."

"I'm not negotiating today." Or ever, with Justin.

"Oh, I think you will." His smile spread and his teeth glowed in this half-light like wolf fangs. "See, we've been researching Maplebrook—and Maplebrook *Farm* in particular. The owner of the orchard seems to be a *special friend* of yours, Emily. In fact, the farm's financial records have been very interesting. Intriguing. Like an *opportunity* we just can't pass up."

My heart chose that moment to shatter. I couldn't pull its shards back together, and they cut against my throat, making my voice crack. "No, Justin. Leave him alone."

"Your friend the failed astronaut seems like the perfect person for us to do business with. We're planning to reach out. Rumor has it, his farm could use a cash infusion. We can provide that."

No. No, no, no. Everything Pokoa and Justin touched at this point would turn to compost. Before, Pokoa Financial had seemed like the goose that laid the golden eggs, but now the gilding was off, and it all just smelled like sulfur.

Rotting, rank, poisonous.

"Leave him alone," I repeated, this time through clenched teeth. "Do not offer him money." The future of the orchard was Buzz's Achilles heel—and they had a poison-tipped arrow aimed straight at it with their bottomless pockets of rescue cash.

"There would be a few conditions."

"Name them. I'll do anything." I couldn't let Buzz get dragged into this. Even if it meant time in jail—or prison, I'd protect him from my past foolish mistakes.

Pokoa spoke at last, telling me exactly what was required of me. Every bullet point on his requirement list was a shovelful of dirt digging my career's grave, as well as my hope of ever being worthy of Buzz's love.

The list was my integrity's death knell.

"I'll do it." My head hung so low it might attract a stray guillotine in the universe.

I've become everything I ever hated.

"Fine. I'll testify the way you request. I'll say nothing to Buzz about this exchange of favors, like you insist." Not that I'd sully him with information about this sordid deal with the devils, anyway. He'd suffered enough in life without having to take on my garbage. "Now, just get away from Maplebrook. I'll mail you my signed statement certified mail. I'll type it up and send it within the hour."

"We'll appreciate it." They exchanged gratified glances. "You've been a lot more compliant than we expected. You must like this farming loser." Justin chuckled like a cartoon villain.

Yes, I'd sacrifice my own integrity—but I'd protect Buzz's no matter what.

"Hey." I reached for the paper and snatched it back. "I said nobody's doing it, but I didn't mean I wouldn't consider it. Who are these people?" *Halston Gregerson, Nora Dinersteen, Rulon Torgerson. Trulia Edmunds.*

"Potential investors in Maplebrook Farm." Emily found a fork on the kitchen countertop and pressed the tines, lifting the handle over and over. "People from businesses around Boston that I've worked with in the past."

Astonishing! "You'd connect me with your contacts? Really?" If it had come a day earlier, I would have crawled to Boston on my knees begging each of these people for a morsel of help. Now, blessedly, I didn't need to. I could ride out the rest of the year in relief, and then after next year's sap season, I could contact them and possibly build something great longer term. Take it slow. I had the leisure of that, thanks to two unexpected investors showing up right there in the orchard this afternoon, brought in on Amos's utility vehicle, like princes handing me bags of gold.

"That's beyond great of you, Emily." I hugged her and then let her go, since she didn't respond like usual. "I might not need this, but thank you all the same. It shows a lot of trust in me." As soon as I had made the balloon payment, I'd give Emily the good news. For now, I'd save the surprise.

"Your sap is a product they might be interested in. Nothing is guaranteed. You'd have to make it appeal to them." She shook her head, frowning. Something had definitely rattled her today, and I didn't think anymore that it was something to do with my past. "Okay, so now you have that. Should we go dance?" Her voice was limp.

"If you're not feeling up to it, we could leave."

"Sorry for being a killjoy tonight."

"Did something happen?"

"Nothing I can talk to you in specific detail about."

"What about in vague detail?" I took her to the dance floor. We slow-danced on a fast song. "I'm a good listener, even if it's vague."

"You are." She danced with me, albeit stiffly.

"Well, well. The cutest couple award goes to Buzz Atchison and Emily France." Coolidge hulked up to us, his bristle-brush mustache twitching. "I should have known romance was the real reason you stole the covered bridge from me. A little bird told me you'll be selling soon, though, and believe me—I'm getting that bridge."

Emily turned to stone in my arms. "What bird?" Her voice quavered.

"None of your beeswax." Coolidge sneered and sashayed to the buffet table.

"I apologize for him." I shot him a return sneer. "He's a revolting human. Please don't consider him representative of the rest of Maplebrook's population."

Emily muttered something I couldn't make out, but it sounded like *No, I'm a revolting human.*

"Emily! It was great to see you at the post office today." Rosie danced over near us. "I was able to get your certified letter in the afternoon's mail truck. Lucky, huh?" Her eyes twinkled at us both. "Buzz, you're in fine form tonight. Like a man in love."

"You may be right." I endured Rosie's pinch of my cheek and ear.

"I can't wait to tell Amos." Rosie giggled and hustled off toward where Amos stood at the punch bowl.

I glanced down at Emily. Had she even heard my oblique admission that I was a man in love? Did she care? "Hey," I nudged again. "Want to hear some good news?"

She snapped back to attention. "Sure. I could use some good news right now." Dejection laced her tone.

"Then you'll love this. I had a couple of entrepreneurs stop by the farm today."

Her eyes bugged out. "No."

"Yep!" I beamed. She did not beam back, but I forged on. "They said they'd sampled Maplebrook Farm's syrup brand, and they loved it. They said it was unique, special, and they offered—"

"No!" Emily shouted, pulling away from me. "Do not take that offer!"

"Em." I took her by the hand and walked her outside into the wintry cold night. "It's amazing for me. Aren't you happy for me? Investors. I can make the balloon payment. I can keep the farm and make my dad happy to be my dad for the first time in thirteen years."

Her attention was everywhere but on me. Her gaze darted all around the recreation center's parking lot. "When did you say they found you? Here? Tonight?"

"Weren't you listening? It was at the orchard in the mid-afternoon." I took her shoulders, slipped my hands down onto her biceps in an attempt to calm her, to gain her attention. "Emily. I just told Rosie I might be in love with you. Can you hear a thing I'm saying? I thought I was the deaf one." I grinned, but she looked at me like I'd just told her I thought her favorite kitten was ugly. *Instead of that I love her.*

"Buzz"—she shook her head, her brows pushing together and her chin bunching up and quivering—"you cannot sign any deal. Don't. I'm begging you."

"Be specific."

"I can't be specific. I'm sorry."

"Then how can I figure out why you don't believe in me all of a sudden?"

"I do believe in you, Buzz. With all my heart, which is why I even—" There was a catch in her throat, and it morphed into a little cry. "I'm sorry. Please, just believe me this once? Don't sign a deal?"

"I signed it at four this afternoon." Worry nagged at me. I batted it away. This was all working out better than I could have dreamed.

"Four o'clock! That was before I even—" She was leaving so many sentences unfinished, so many things unsaid and unexplained.

I couldn't take it. "I'll listen to anything you're willing to tell me, but you need to know that I'm finally free of the balloon payment. I'm ready to move forward on lots of things in life, if you're willing to walk down those trails with me, Emily. I don't want to go down them alone."

There! I'd poured it all out there, laid my heart on the ground in front of her in a pulsating, vulnerable mass.

And next, she kicked dirt on it.

"Take me back to the Bridge Cottage. I'm sorry, but I have to go."

Chapter 15

Emily

The fire in the pot-belly stove had gone out, and I couldn't for the life of me get it to start again. I tried time and again, but every match and every bit of kindling seemed soaked, as if someone had poured ten gallons of water on all the fuel.

I slammed the little iron door shut. Patting my upper arms, I paced the room to get warm. Buzz had been nothing but ice to me as he'd taken me home. No words were spoken between us on the whole drive from the village.

What could be said? He'd unwittingly allowed himself to be bought and paid for by criminals. He was now under their power. His orchard's good name and reputation was tied indelibly to theirs. If Pokoa Financial went down, they could broadcast his orchard as one of their investments, and his family name would be sullied. No one would want Maplebrook Farm's syrup, and he'd be out of business.

If he knew that I'd led those crooks to his doorstep and endangered the orchard's future, he'd never forgive me.

Nor should he.

Meanwhile, like a naïve fool, I'd complied with their wishes—to protect Buzz. Sick and numb, I'd mailed a sworn affidavit, too, stating that Justin and Pokoa were innocent in the fraudulent actions, the insider trading scam, and in everything else. I'd signed and dated and even fingerprinted in ink my statement that I was the sole guilty party in the scheme, absolving them and all other company employees of culpability.

I'd been vehement in my writing.

No judge could ignore it.

No, Buzz, I wouldn't be spending the winter in Maplebrook. Instead, I'd be spending it at Club Fed like Dad. Or worse. They might not send me to the posh-version of prison for non-violent criminals. Justin and Pokoa might lobby behind the scenes for me to land in a truly heinous location.

It would have been worth it if I really could have saved Buzz from their schemes. If only I'd known they'd already gotten their hooks into him, I never would have confessed to a crime I didn't commit.

I never should have come to Maplebrook. Then, Buzz could have lived on at his orchard, happier than if he'd never met me because he wouldn't have the threat of losing his livelihood and his family's legacy. A way to make the balloon payment would have occurred to him—surely. He was the type who figured things out, who made sacrifices to succeed.

Now that I can keep the orchard going, my dad will finally be happy to be my dad for the first time in thirteen years.

That statement that Buzz had made while we were at the Christmas party. Ugh. It was like the final puzzle piece locking into place so that I could see the whole picture of Buzz's motivation for investing in Maplebrook Farm. When he'd been injured at survival school and forced out of the astronaut training program, he'd botched his dad's dream of his sons both becoming space jockeys. *Everything Buzz had done to save Maplebrook had been to win his dad's approval.* Wince! I could see it as plain as stars in a country night sky.

Well, at least in my case, approval from fathers could definitely be overrated.

Like father like daughter, though. My apple certainly hadn't fallen very far from the tree, had it? Or, so the court records would show. In fact, maybe they'd give me the cell adjacent to Dad's old digs. Wouldn't that be nostalgic?

If I changed a single thing in my testimony, if I retracted even a hair, Justin and Pokoa now had the power to sully Maplebrook Farm's reputation. Snap! It could be gone, and the village could turn on him. Amos, too. Worse, they could take him to court for any trumped-up reason, use their extensive legal connections and bottomless bank accounts, and sue him into the ground. They had their hooks into him, deep.

If only Buzz could decipher and follow the oblique suggestions I'd scribbled on the papers I'd given to him! But I couldn't hint beyond that level, at least not about Justin or Mr. Pokoa. I'd signed the blasted nondisclosure agreement, and done everything else they'd demanded—and they'd not only come after Buzz hardcore, they'd probably seek and destroy anyone else in my family or friends they could locate.

I'd done enough damage.

Tonight, at the holiday kickoff party, Buzz had more or less told the world he was in love with me. He'd thought I hadn't heard him! The words had been nectar to my parched, sugar-crashing soul. And yet, in that moment—how could I have even responded verbally? Could I have told him the truth? That I'd fallen for him so hard that I was willing to give up everything I'd ever known, everything I cherished—for him and his future?

If only I hadn't been forced into silence so that he wouldn't know that I'd led him into a tangled web that endangered his livelihood and his family's good name.

The back of my throat closed, making a hiccup sound. Something was getting the collar of my blouse wet. I tapped it with my forefinger. Oh, no surprise. Those were tears.

In my purse I found a notepad and a pen. After three failed scrawls to get the ink flowing in this ice chamber, it finally worked. I penned

Buzz a letter. Besides a few apologies and heartfelt wishes for his happiness, and one oblique reference to the nudges I'd given him about maple water, I'd just written my second not-in-person break-up message this year.

My manners could use some work.

So much for hope of my first-snowfall wish ever coming true.

I packed a few things, turned off the lights, and locked up Bridge Cottage.

Goodbye.

Chapter 16

Buzz

"Where's your pretty blonde girlfriend?" Van manned the register at The Furniture Store.

Instead of answering, I placed my recent purchase on the counter. "I have my receipt. Do you take returns?"

Greta came over, her hands full of a tray of holiday cupcakes. "Oh, sugar. That's such a shame. I heard she went back to town."

Had she? How would I know? All I had left of her was the Bridge Cottage, memories, and the note in her precise handwriting.

Don't come find me. Be well. Know that I'm a better person for having known you, Buzz. You're the best man of my acquaintance. Please, please stay that way.

"Son," Van said, "forgive me, but on jewelry we have a no-return policy."

"Van!" Greta stomped her foot, making a cupcake quake on the tray. "That's not—"

"It's true in this case. Sorry, Buzz. You'll have to hang onto that."

Greta grumbled something I couldn't quite make out and bustled away.

I left. Sure, it was obvious—Van was a romantic, telling me he wouldn't take the ring back on the expectation that Emily would return.

Emily wasn't coming back.

Back home, I sat in my truck and stared at the bridge for a long time. It looked colder now, despite the fact the weather had turned warm, just as the almanac had predicted.

Finally, I went inside the house. I pulled a random book off the shelf, glanced at the Robert Frost poem about nothing gold being able to stay. How true, and how sad. And how true.

After a while, I got out her notes again, the papers she'd given me the last happy day, whenever that had been. Felt like a million years ago.

Forty degrees daytime temp. Twenties at night.

Halston Gregerson, Nora Dinersteen, Rulon Torgerson. Trulia Edmunds.

Maple water=coconut water.

The words on the middle line were the contacts she'd given me to reach out to if I decided to pivot my business plan next spring. Well, just to honor Emily's memory and not let her parting generosity go to waste, I called up the first person on the list, giving my name, telling them Emily had recommended them, and left a number.

In turn, I called the other three, same message. There. I'd done something with it.

My phone chirped a temperature alert. Man, how could last Monday's high have been negative four and today we were sitting at forty-four degrees Fahrenheit? It was practically spring.

My heart felt nothing like spring. It was the dead of winter in there. Emphasis on dead.

Emily, I just … miss you. I miss us. I miss me with you.

I needed to blow my nose. Something must be in my eye, because it was leaking like crazy. Both of them were. And I was out of Kleenex. I'd taken my tissue box over to Bridge Cottage the day Emily moved in. Now, I did the manly thing and used my shirt's sleeve.

Where was she? I did what I swore I wouldn't do again, and I got online and searched her name. Again, the Pokoa Financial case came up first—but this time, it came with photos of all the accused fraudsters. Emily's face was largest, at the very top. A javelin to my soul! She looked so stoic in the photo, like she was standing for something—and not like she was remorseful, since she obviously wasn't guilty.

On the surface, anyone else seeing it might consider it ironic—her constant insistence on integrity. Harping on it at times, actually. And now, this accusation. Of course, she had done this all with some purpose. If only I knew what it could be.

Meanwhile, because she'd come to Maplebrook, I'd fallen in love with her. If there was anything I could do in the whole world to make this right for her, I'd do it.

I needed a solution.

A glutton for punishment, I scrolled a little lower to read the news article, but instead my eyes jumped right out of their sockets. That face! The next *two* faces, in fact. I'd seen them. These were men I'd met, shaken hands with—*taken an investment from.*

My whole house turned on its side, and my head started ringing. It was worse than that crunching pain and shock when I'd landed at the bottom of the ravine—but in this moment my right femur ached just as badly as it had all through that terrible night.

Heaven help me! I'd accepted a massive investment from two of the accused criminals in Emily's company. With that much money involved, they could do almost anything to Maplebrook Farm. Or to me.

Sickness roiled in me. She'd warned me. Of course, at the time it'd been too late, but she'd told me not to do it. *Why hadn't she been forthcoming about why?*

I bit the inside of my cheek and scrolled to their names. I opened the pictures app on my phone and scrolled to the photo I'd taken of the cashier's check they'd handed me. Justin Marchwell and Nico Pokoa. Same as the captions on the photos, their beady, criminal eyes stared out, mocking me from the screen.

I sat back on the office chair, my head flopping over the top of it, and stared at the ceiling. It seemed to get farther away and closer, over and over again.

This could not go on! I had to stop that check!

I ran out to my truck.

Fifteen minutes later, I was pounding on Yves's office door. "It's five-oh-five, Yves, I know you're still in there." His slick banker's car, as Amos would call it, sat in the parking lot. "Come on, Yves. I need you. It's an emergency."

The door cracked open. "I'd guess it was an emergency or you wouldn't be hollering like you've got a porcupine stuck in your leg." He let me in. "What on earth is the matter with you? I thought we were square since you paid your balloon payment. Cool your jets. You're set."

"That's just it. The balloon payment. Did you cash that check already? If not, can I have it back?"

Yves threw his head back and gut-laughed. "You gave me that money five days ago, buddy. I put it in the account within five minutes of your driving off in debt-reduction glee."

"It's gone, then?" My mouth got dry. "I can't get it back?" I said with sand in my throat. "I have to have it back."

Yves just shook his head. "I can't help you with that, man."

"Then, can you *lend* me that exact amount—just temporarily—and I'll pay you back absolutely positively no later than the thirty-first?" Of course, I had no sure plan of how I'd get it by then, but I'd find a way no matter what. Anything to get out from under the thumb of Emily's oppressors. *And maybe to help Emily be free of them, too.* My conscience whispered that Maplebrook Farm had something to do with why she was in the trouble she faced.

When Yves looked at me like I'd taken a bite out of the porcupine stuck to my leg, I pushed my case harder. "Whether you get the money now or then, it ends up being exactly the same net sum. Do the numbers."

Three disbelief-filled blinks later, he held the door open for me again and shooed me out. "Merry Christmas, Buzz. I'm not sure what's going on with you, but best wishes. And a happy New Year." The door clanked shut.

I stood in the semi-cold, my blood coagulating in my veins.

What were my options? What, what, what? My eyes darted here and there on the street of Maplebrook village. Anyone? Something? Help? Nothing, no one could help me. I sank against the door of my truck, my hand in a fist pounding the side of my head as if it would jar an idea loose. A solution-type idea.

In a haze, I drove home and plopped down at my kitchen table with only the flier from the sawmill—which I'd wadded up and meant to throw in the trash—and the few papers from Emily scattered in front of me.

Sawmill. If I sold the trees, I'd be able to pay back the loan. I wouldn't have dirty money on my hands. I could tell those Pokoa Financial chumps to stick it, and I could get word to Emily that I'd finally seen what she was talking about—she'd told me in no uncertain terms I shouldn't take any investors. I'd already done it, but I'd had no idea they were shysters of the blackest dye.

Sawmill.

The trees would all have to go to lumber, eventually, as the fine print on the flier requested full access to every tree—although I'd keep the deed to the property.

You can replant, they said. Grow another crop.

I stared at the phone number, and then picked up and dialed.

Chapter 17

Buzz

"I'm sorry. I must have the wrong number." I hung up on the sawmill's receptionist the second she answered.

My soul recoiled at the idea. Great-grandpa had referred to it as a farm, but I don't think he meant the trees themselves as the product to be cut down and sold.

Yes, I'd do anything to pay back the money—but could I figure out something that didn't involve destroying my dad's childhood, and my family's legacy, and my future income?

I would keep thinking. No problem was too great that it could withstand sustained thinking.

If not, I'd have to come back to this. But for now, I folded it over and stuck it at the bottom of the pile.

What lay there next in the pile was Emily's no-nonsense handwriting.

Forty degrees daytime temp. Twenties at night.

Just like this weird week. Huh. Had she been prophesying the weather? Well, then she was better than Yuseff's almanac.

Just a minute. Just a minute! If the temps were exactly right—and they had been for the past three days—I could tap.

The sap was running. Right now!

"Amos! Amos!" I shoved my arm into my jacket's sleeve as I skittered down the porch steps and raced toward the tool shed. "Amos! You out there?"

Amos shambled into view on the far side of the shed. "You all right, Buzz? You're all excited-like. First time since your girl left."

"That girl who used to be mine is a genius!" I shook Amos by the shoulders.

"Could'a told you that myself." Amos rolled his eyes like a teen girl. "My sister Rosie said a couple things about your Emily lately. First off, her last name ain't France. It's England."

"Easy to get confused, there."

"Right?" Amos gave a deep nod as he grabbed a couple of drills off the shelf—even before I'd told him what I was up to. "Second, she said Greta came by with a big fancy flier with a drawing of the covered bridge on it. For sale."

For sale! "No!" Emily couldn't be selling the bridge! It was our memories together. Did she not care about them anymore? That sick feeling roiled in me again. "Did she say why?" Maybe she had to pay court fees. Maybe ... I couldn't think of any reason why she'd give it up other than she was giving me up.

"Nobody knows why. Not for sure. I jes' hope she doesn't sell it to Coolidge."

Well, I wouldn't let her. I was going to fight for the woman I love.

"Greta has heard from her, it seems." Amos chewed a thumbnail.

"I'm glad someone's been in touch with her." Sort of. Emily had called Greta, but she hadn't called me. It stung, but I could understand. I'd betrayed her trust—unwittingly—by taking that money from her vile coworkers. In fact, by doing so, I'd put myself under their thumbs. There was a strong chance they'd been using me to manipulate Emily.

Maybe she does love me.

"What else did Rosie say about Emily?"

Please let it be that she sent a message that she still loves me.

But, no. Not that, and nothing good.

"Rosie also said she read all about your girl and her big confession. Seems like she'd got herself into trouble by the tonnage." He scratched the side of his head. "Funny, though. It don't seem likely that Miss Emily had much if anything to confess. To tattle on, sure. I can sure-as-rain picture her telling about someone else's sneaky moves. Rosie said that Emily, quote, *gave up her immunity and confessed.* What do you think that means?"

Confessed! Gave up immunity? But she'd been hiding from those people, who must have threatened her. The terrible picture was coming together—of her wrenching choice and situation.

I needed to find her. I had to do something to make it right, and I had to beg her forgiveness for not listening to her counsel, for not trusting her enough in the moment, and for letting her go.

However, I had to figure out how to *not* owe those crooks tens of thousands of dollars first. I grabbed a drill, my five-gallon bucket of taps that had been sterilized just last week, and I jumped in the side-by-side.

Amos was already strapped in. "We doing an autumn tap like your girl suggested?"

"You knew she'd had that idea?"

"Course. I gave her the idea."

Maybe so, maybe not. "Can the two of us get enough sap to make a dent in how much I'll need? What do you think?"

"Maybe. You could call in some help."

True. Maybe other sap gatherers in town wouldn't be out bow-hunting this week, since it was so warm. *Doubtful.* But they might take pity on me and show up.

"You could always call up your dad. See if he wants to relive his childhood."

That idea was all Amos. And it wasn't half bad. "I'll call him up right now." I reached for my phone, but just then, as were rumbling into the orchard in our open jalopy, my phone dinged a text. It was from the

Trulia Edmunds person.

Any investment idea that Emily England recommends is something I'm buying. I'll be there at dawn to see the place and the potential. Please send address.

All the hairs on my arms raised and my legs tingled. This was going to work! Thanks to Emily, I was going to be able to get myself out of hock—and maybe, somehow, release her from those legal clutches and free up her conscience about dragging those crooks to Maplebrook as well.

"Let's get a move on, Amos."

Chapter 18

Emily

"It's the week before Christmas, Emily," my lawyer Jerry said, pleading with me in a stage whisper in the otherwise empty courtroom. "You can't make me let them put you in jail. How do you think I'll be able to enjoy the holiday with my wife and kids if you're rotting in jail on Christmas?"

The courtroom would be full in a matter of minutes. It was too late for Jerry to be persuading me. I'd made up my mind. I was protecting Buzz.

"I won't be the first England to spend a holiday in the clink." I smirked. Jerry had been Dad's lawyer, too. But he'd had to defend a guilty man in those days. "It'll feel like family bonding for me. Besides, I won't be rotting until at least *next* Christmas, since rot takes time to set in. You can enjoy this one with Martha and the kids."

He paced the space in front of the table for the defense, pulling at his hair, which was a mistake, since he wore a toupee.

"It's not too late. You can simply retract your statement that you *mailed to opposing counsel without telling me*. Thanks for the vote of confidence, by the way. The judge will understand. Anyone with a brain will read that verbiage and see that it was written under duress. Even your handwriting is wobbly, and your signature looks like you had a gun pointed to your head at the time. It's clearly a blackmail situation." He lowered his voice even further—to a level Buzz wouldn't have been able to discern if he'd been here. "Whom are you protecting?"

"I love that you use whom. Very correct grammar," I deflected. "Forget it, Jerry. You're going to have to deal with the blot on your record of allowing two Englands to go to jail."

"What about the life you made for yourself in Vermont?" Jerry lowered his voice. "I got the distinct impression you were happy there. Didn't you buy something? Property?"

"It's being sold. I had an easy buyer."

A flurry sounded at the back of the room, and the double doors flew open. In walked the two last people I ever wanted to see again in my life, followed by a host of other former colleagues from Pokoa Financial. It looked like the SEC had assembled a cast of *usual suspects.*

Justin looked as confident and handsome as ever in his two-thousand-dollar suit—with a side of smugness in his pocket square. Mr. Pokoa's diamond cuff-links caught the lights and glinted in my eyes.

Slick.

I used to be more like them, with my slick car. Now, I wanted nothing to do with them or anyone like them. Ever again.

Jerry harrumphed. "The nerve of those people to waltz in here with those smug, triumphant looks on their faces, when they *know* they only get off scot free because they've got a knife's tip digging into your spine." Jerry muttered some more things, which might have included some unpleasant names for my former coworkers.

As other spectators filed in, Justin and Mr. Pokoa took seats near the back. They weren't the first defendants of the day, and they were pleading not guilty. Everyone, including me, including them, expected their cases to be dismissed perfunctorily once my evidence was presented to the judge. I'd be taking a hundred percent of the responsibility for the wrongdoing.

My guts twisted like they were on a carnival ride.

"All rise." The bailiff was a tall, stern-looking guy with a flat-top haircut. *Like Buzz's.* For the first time today, emotion slapped me hard. My eyes stung, and I blinked back the evidence that I was giving up my hopes of Bridge Cottage and of the farmhouse at Maplebrook Farm with Buzz, forever.

That dream floated away, like ashes from an urn.

Justin came forward, leaned over the railing, and hissed in my ear. "Smart of you to look sexy for the judge today."

"Back away, Marchwell." Jerry whirled on him with a murderous look in his eye. I swear, his irises turned a glowing red. "If you talk to my client one more time, I'll have security put you on the floor with a knee in your back."

Justin raised his palms in surrender and backed off. But he obviously couldn't resist getting in one last dig. "Fine, fine. I was just going to say what a shame it was that her boyfriend couldn't see her looking so nice in a color other than orange one last time."

Jerry nearly hurdled the fence between the defense table and the gallery, his hands shaped in a loop ready to choke the bloke. Acting fast, I grabbed at Jerry's suit-coat jacket, yanking him back to our side of the banister.

"Heel, Jerry. He's toothless if I don't care what he thinks." I honestly didn't care what Justin thought. He'd gone from being the brightest star in my sky to the blackest spot in the universe to ... nothing. A big, fat, ball of apathy-inducing nothing.

The judge entered.

My fate was sealed.

Chapter 19

Buzz

I drove like the wind—as windy as I could get in the Boston traffic, that was. Five days ago, I'd handed over the first large delivery of maple water to Trulia Edmunds. Based on an agreement to take this season's maple water, plus a promise of quadruple the amount of even sweeter raw sap—maple water—around March, she'd fronted a portion of the springtime payment, as well. The check from Trulia ended up being double the amount I owed those criminals who'd been exercising power over Emily. I'd read all about the trial on the news, glued myself to every update, ever since Amos had told me what was really going on.

The online news report told me little I actually needed to know, but I could piece together the rest.

I would have been in Boston with the repayment the second I received the check, but it had taken five full business days for Yves's banking connections to release the funds for an amount that large—which made sense, rules-wise, but I'd been going completely berserk ever since while waiting. Her trial date had inched closer, and I still didn't have the funds.

"The moneys are available!" Yves's phone call at three minutes after seven this morning shot me straight into my truck and out the door toward Yves's office, where he handed over the cash.

If I sped, I'd make the ten o'clock court time.

The cash burned in the breast pocket of my jacket as I rolled pedal-to-the-metal all the way into the city, the closest I'd come to flying since I left the Air Force. Despite traffic's diabolical effort to keep me away, I screeched into the Suffolk County courthouse parking lot with only seconds to spare. I leaped from the truck, the envelope of cash crushing in my fist.

"Judge Wixom's court?" I asked as I pushed through the security checkpoint.

The bored guard answered in monotone, "Third floor."

I skipped the elevator, which might be slow, and hot-footed it to the stairwell, taking two steps at a time all the way to the third floor. I burst through the doors and jogged to the courtroom, just as an usher was shutting the door.

"Wait! Hold up!" I yelled. "Is that Judge Wixom's courtroom?"

The usher stepped aside to avoid my body's impersonation of a runaway freight train. "Justin Marchwell! Nico Pokoa! Stop whatever you're thinking right now, you blackmailing"—I added a choice term as I burst into the room and shot toward those lying jerks. "Here's your extortion funds returned to you in full. Count every dollar." I shoved the envelope at Justin, resisting the urge to punch him right in the nose. "I knew you'd be here. You wouldn't be able to resist watching her cover up your lies for you, to watch her go down in flames while you chuckled safe in your tower. But your tower is made of ice, and ice melts when the sun comes out and shines on the dark places."

I was really on a roll. So much so, that I hardly noticed when two men in uniform hooked me by both arms and dragged me back out the door of the courtroom. The door slammed.

I hadn't even seen Emily, other than a brief, peripheral glimpse of her beautiful face looking shocked and—was it horrified or amazed? I didn't know.

However, I'd come and done what I had intended to do: to relieve myself of any obligation to those fraudsters, and to prove to Emily in person and loudly that she needn't owe them a single iota of loyalty on my account.

Someone in uniform was asking me for my name. They seemed like they were considering booking me into custody for disorderly conduct. I waved them off. "Don't worry, guys. I'm not a threat to myself or anyone else at this point. I'll go quietly back to my country life now."

Just then, the courtroom doors flew open, and a host of people exited at once, grumbling about a postponement of the hearing.

I peeked into the room. My two *investors* were huddled with some attorneys who Amos would say looked like the type that might also represent casino owners, gold chains and slicked-back hairstyles and all. Yells tumbled out into the echoing hallway. None of it sounded happy.

Someone approached me. "You were out of order, young man." A fellow in a suit—sporting the worst toupee I'd seen since … ever—came up and offered to shake my hand. "Way out of order."

"I'm sorry, sir." Why was he pumping my hand like he could get groundwater to spout from it? "The hearing was postponed?"

"Yep. Until the rest of the evidence can be reviewed." The guy grinned like he'd just been told he'd won a billion dollars. "I'm Jerry McCormick, Emily's lawyer. I take it you're the reason she confessed to the crime?" He looked me over. "If my wife were here, she'd tell you she could see why Emily was so insistent."

I could have puzzled out his meaning, but just then, Emily shot out of the courtroom and launched herself straight into my arms. I pulled her tight, lifted her up, and spun in a circle. I was home. Together, we were *home.*

"I'm selling the maple water, like you suggested."

"Trulia told me. At least, I thought that was what she'd said." Emily still hadn't unburied her face from my chest, so I had to guess at her statement. As if remembering my hearing problem, she looked up at me and grinned. "She's excited. This could be the next big thing. They have a label ready and everything."

"Does that mean you want to come and help me with the sap run? We've got perfect sap weather."

"You're the perfect sap." She patted my chest and laughed, but then, she tilted her head and spoke thoughtfully. "I take that back. You're my hero."

I was? *To her, I could be.*

Chapter 20

Buzz

Outside, the weather was cold if not snowy, but inside? It was just right—because Emily sat beneath my arm, her head against my chest.

"Christmas Eve in front of the fire." Emily put her feet up on the coffee table in the farmhouse living room. "It's warm in here."

"With you beside me, I'll never be cold." I grinned. "How's that for perfect sap?" I hadn't let her live that pun down for the last entire week we'd spent in the woods.

"Who's sappy?" In walked Mom, bearing a tray of baked goods from The Furniture Store. Dad followed, reaching over her shoulder and snitching a scone.

"We all are, now that we've collected from a third of your great-grandparents' orchard. We'll save the other two-thirds for you young folks to handle next spring." Dad stretched and laced his hands behind his head.

Mom sat down on the loveseat near the window. "It's great to spend Christmas in the country for once. The city is so hectic. I'm loving this. I heard it might even snow."

"Where did you hear that?" I asked. The news hadn't mentioned anything about snow.

"I ran into some excitable fellow while I was shopping for groceries." Mom set down the tray. "He kept waving the almanac in my face like he thought he was Nostradamus."

Mom wore her famous red Christmas sweater, the one with the Scottie dog on the front and the plaid collar. Dad wore the matching green sweater she insisted on. They were quite the pair, married more than thirty-five years now. Growing old together like two hearts beating in the same breast.

I want that.

"Know what I think?" Dad sat down on the loveseat and stretched his arm around Mom's shoulders. "We should locate that one perfect tree again and finally build that tree house."

Emily sat up and reached for him, waving her hands. "I know that tree! The very one!"

Dad looked at her with shock and then approval. Then, he gave me a similar look. It hit me like a stray model rocket to the chest. *He's pleased with me.*

"What's that surprised look?" he asked me.

"I don't know." I shrugged. It wasn't like I'd tell my dad I always thought he believed I was a slouch, a major disappointment—especially not with Emily listening.

"Son," Dad said. "I don't know if we've ever expressed it clearly enough, but your mom and I were so proud of you for being so resilient after your accident. You just got up and went right back to work—exemplifying the Atchison way. You didn't let any of that discourage you from soldiering on. And then, when the family needed you, you stepped in and helped out my aunt and uncle. You've lived your life like we always knew you would—with heroism. You're a good example to Neil. And to us."

"To Neil?" The hero? "You're joking."

"Not at all. Every time we talk to him, he asks how you are, and mentions he wants to be like you someday."

Nuh-uh. My world just turned on its side and went rolling down a steep hill. When it stopped at the bottom, it finally felt right. Dad had meant it. Every word.

While the conversation rattled on, I sat beside Emily, soaking up the meaning of it all. Mom and Dad, proud of me. Neil's example.

And without Emily, I might never have had this conversation.

"Hey, think of this. We'll be here a couple more days," Dad said. "Is there lumber on the property? Enough around that we could at least get started on that tree house again? We could all do it together. Childhood dream come true—thanks to the fact you saved this orchard for our family."

"You're a hero to us, Buzz." Mom reached over and patted my foot, which was all she could reach from her spot on the loveseat.

"Indeed," Dad said, shooting yet another missile at my soul. *They think I'm a hero.* "You know, there are some things that last."

"Like maple trees?" Emily asked. "I heard there are some older than the U.S. Constitution on this property."

"Yes," Dad said, looking at me. "And like family."

The tree house. I was finally going to do it—and with Dad. A deep spot inside my lungs exhaled.

For the next hour or so, Emily and Dad drew up blueprints for the tree house. I ate more scones than a human should in one sitting. Mom sat at the piano and played "Silent Night," and we all came over and stood around to sing. We made it through "Hark, the Herald Angels," "The First Noel," "We Three Kings," and about a dozen more before Mom's arthritis set us free.

"Son," Dad said later as he and I took the trash out to the burn barrel, "you've really done something amazing with this orchard. Thanks for letting Mom and me come and be part of the frenzy of activity this past week. I had no idea how fun it could be. Mom said we should leave it to the young people, but all this talk of a tree house is taking decades off me. Let us do the sap run with you next year."

"As in late February, early March?"

"Whenever the temperature is right. I'm retired, and all I have to rejoice in is my two heroic sons—and their children." He gave me one of those obvious, obnoxious winks.

I'd take all the obnoxious winks he aimed at me. They were the food of my long-hungry soul.

"Working on it, Dad." I patted my jacket pocket where my non-returnable item from The Furniture Store's jewelry case lay, waiting for the right moment and place.

In the moonlight, the covered bridge winked at me, too.

Chapter 21

Emily

Clouds gathered on New Year's Eve. The weather forecast threatened to pack all of Maplebrook deep in a white blanket. I couldn't wait to wake up tomorrow morning and see the clouds' and fog's handiwork, with my bridge arrayed like a bride in sparkling satin. For now, however, everyone in Maplebrook gathered on the covered bridge and counted down to midnight, still under a snow-less sky.

"Five, four, three, two, one. Happy New Year!" Party hats flew into the air, and kisses smacked in the night. "Should auld acquaintance be forgot …"

It was the sweetest New Year's Eve of my life, surrounded by the good people of Maplebrook.

"Well, well," a sneering voice interrupted Buzz's and my toast.

Okay, not everyone in Maplebrook was sweet. "Hello, Mr. Coolidge. Happy New Year."

"That's what you say, when you baited me about selling your property! Then, you went and subdivided it, selling only the worthless shack and keeping the bridge for yourself. I should sue you for false advertising."

Um, it didn't work like that. "What are your plans for the new year, Mr. Coolidge?"

"I'm going to buy and renew a *different* bridge, I'll have you know. Someday, I'll be known as the man who saved all the covered bridges in New England!"

Amos strolled up to us. "Ah, say. Mr. Coolidge. Can I talk to you about *preservation* of covered bridges? It's a whole different ball of wax compared to *restoration*. It's way more prestigious and expensive."

To all our surprise, Coolidge looked intrigued. "More prestigious? More expensive?"

"Much. You'd be re-*nowned* in the whole bloomin' state if you got yourself involved in preservation."

Coolidge narrowed his eyes and then relaxed them. "You've got me listening. Do you have any contacts in the preservation community you could introduce me to?"

"Oh, yes. And you'd be their rising star."

Coolidge's triumphant laugh shook the night.

The party went on for another half hour, and then villagers trickled away.

Buzz and I were left alone on the bridge, once again. Just like that night of our first kiss.

I liked it best this way. This was Buzz's and my place, no matter who all claimed it as their own.

"Nothing like New Year's Eve parties." I gripped Buzz's hand for solidity and warmth. The weather was chilly. "Too bad they didn't leave the heat lamps when they cleared away everything else."

"I'll keep you warm." Buzz pulled me into a hug. Buzz Atchison officially gave the world's best hugs. This one was in competition for first place Best Hug Ever, but it was hard to beat the one he'd managed at the courthouse a couple of weeks ago when he'd altered my future and saved me from perjuring myself in court.

Bless him.

"The bridge should seem deserted without the entire population of the town," I said through chattering teeth, "but it's funny that with you here, I could never feel lonely. You're the missing part of me."

All that remained was a lot of stray confetti, a cork, and the two of us—plus the babbling of the stream. Well, and the covered bridge itself. It seemed to have a personality, a character all its own.

This bridge had been, in some magical way, our matchmaker.

"When do you close on the sale of Bridge Cottage?" Buzz asked. "Six weeks?"

"Right on Valentine's Day. Van and Greta are going to get super-host status instantly, I'll bet." They planned on turning our little renovated bungalow into a bed and breakfast. They'd made me an offer I shouldn't refuse, even though I'd miss my little home terribly.

Of course, they'd also mentioned keeping it a few years until Buzz's dad retired and then seeing whether Mr. and Mrs. Atchison would like to move back to Maplebrook.

I gazed at the glowing windows of Brook Cottage that invited me home—a home I'd never belong to again. "I'm not sure where I'll land next."

"How about I make a suggestion?" Buzz placed his gloves on my cheek and turned my face toward him. "It's a job offer."

"Oh?" Being out of a job for the past few months, I guess this shouldn't come as a shock to me. "What kind of job?"

"Assistant orchard farmer."

"Buzz. I don't know. It might hurt Amos's feelings."

"Okay, then how about this?" Buzz dropped to one knee, its fall echoing on the wood slat of the bridge.

"Buzz—what in—?" Then my mouth clamped shut, and my heart shifted into overdrive. "Is this?"

"Uh-huh." Buzz grinned up at me. "It's the scariest moment of my life, if that's what you were going to ask."

Ahhh! My insides screamed. I stood on the covered bridge, the kissing bridge, the very spot where I'd first kissed Buzz Atchison, where I'd seen him and fallen instantly in like with him, and now where

I was far-gone in love with him.

"Emily England." He cleared his throat a few times, gazing up at me with those gorgeous hazel eyes.

He had prepared a speech! This moment's incarnation was better than I'd even dreamed!

"From the moment we met on this covered bridge, I wanted to kiss you. From the moment I kissed you on this covered bridge, I was head-over-heels in love with you. Your compassion, your ability to see me for who I am, to draw me out of my hiding place while you yourself were in hiding, your intelligent problem-solving, your kiss—I could go on for hours about the many things that have hurtled me toward this moment. I'm yours. Please, will you take the job offer of being … my wife?"

From his pocket, he produced a ring. The simple, antique diamond caught a glint from a moonbeam, or maybe from a planet's starlight. I held out my hand so he could slip it onto my ring finger. It fit like a dream.

"It's perfect," I whispered because my vocal cords had taken a trip to outer space.

"That's a yes?" He looked up at me so earnestly, so full of integrity and strength. The man for me! He stood.

"It's yes. Buzz, I'm yours." I swatted at a tear, and a winter gust brought a flurry of snowflakes between the lattice of the bridge. The first snowfall!

One snowflake landed on my cheek.

"Buzz?" I asked. "Remember when you asked me why I wanted to buy a covered bridge?"

"Yeah."

"This is why."

I kissed my hero once again. My long ago first-snowfall wish had come true.

Epilogue

Emily

My bridal shower was in full swing under a silk tent on the back lawn of Seacliff Chateau. Mallory, Jayne, and I—plus a few relatives and friends we could bring together at the last minute since Buzz and I didn't leave much leeway between our engagement and our wedding—were all here with me to celebrate my nuptials tomorrow.

Mallory had even roped a college friend into being our photographer. Beatrix was dutifully snapping photos of us as we made dumb faces, as I opened gifts of all kinds—from crock pots to lingerie to a fire extinguisher.

"Buzz and I will not be extinguishing fires. We intend only to light them." I shook the red canister. Everyone laughed at my stupid joke.

Eventually, all our moms and aunts took off. Only Jayne, Mallory, the photographer, and I remained with the piles of wrapping paper and my nerves about tomorrow.

I'm marrying Buzz. He's going to be good to me. I shouldn't be nervous.

"Here comes the bride," Mallory sang off key, swinging up her cup of cocoa like she was a German during Oktoberfest. "All fat and wide."

"Hey!" I shoved her other arm. "What's that about?"

"I'm singing about myself, girl." She patted her rounding belly. "It was only a year ago I was the one standing on the back lawn of this house as the bride. Now look at me."

"Mallory does blush prettily as a mother-to-be," Jayne said. Mallory and Calder had wasted no time in starting their family. Of course, that was what she had always wished for—a happier, more stable upbringing than her own.

With Calder, she had found it.

With Buzz, so would I. "Maybe Buzz and I will join your time frame." Buzz would make the most adorable father. I could picture him already, holding our babies, taking them out in the orchard. *Building a tree house with them. Maybe even one for each of them.*

Forever with Buzz seemed so full of possibilities.

"And to think, we all got our first-snowfall wishes." Jayne bounced her little Albany on her lap to keep her asleep. "Every one of us!"

"What's that?" Beatrix lowered her camera and asked. "First-snowfall wish, did you say? I never heard about that one in any of our folklore classes."

Mallory waved it off. "It's not something they're going to teach in school. It's far too black magic for that."

Black magic! "Mallory." I elbowed her. Pregnancy was making her a little crazy. "Quit it. There's nothing dark about it." I pulled Beatrix down to sit on the Adirondack chair beside me. "Here's what happened."

I described the cabin where my grandparents had taken the three of us for a holiday vacation when we were sixteen. "It was a gorgeous night, cloudy with just one area of the clouds glowing where the moon shone. My grandma came out and told us, 'If it does snow, and they say it will, catch the first snowflake you see.'"

"And?" Beatrix almost sounded breathless, as if this mattered to her deeply. "And what happened? Did you catch them?"

I looked at Jayne. Jayne looked at Mallory. Mallory looked at me.

"We caught them," I said.

Beatrix closed her eyes, as if savoring this. "You made a wish, didn't you?" Her eyes flew wide. "Was it a wish on love? And did it come true for all of you?"

Were we that transparent? "Exactly," I said.

With extreme earnestness, Beatrix leaned toward Jayne. "What did you wish for? And you, Mallory? What about you?" She looked at me. "You said it worked?"

It took some crazy explanation, but Jayne told about her wish for our hottie English teacher, Mr. Deloitte—and how her own wish had nearly blinded her, but how it had ultimately come full circle, thanks to her husband's eventual career change.

"The weird thing is," Mallory said, "I ended up randomly meeting the guy Jayne originally assumed was the fulfillment of her wish." She laughed hysterically for a little bit too long. If she hadn't been pregnant and staying away from alcohol, I would have thought she was tipsy the way she giggled. "But I can't imagine Jayne being happy with my guy."

"Yeah, the whole time I was with him, I kept thinking, *this guy should meet Mallory.*" Jayne looked like she wanted to throw cold water on Mallory for the noisy laughter that might wake Baby Albany. "It all worked out, though. The wishes knew how to sort themselves."

Beatrix already knew a little about Mallory's original wish for a prince.

"And you?" Beatrix asked. "I would never have expected you, Emily England, of Boston financial world fame, to wish for a sugar maple farmer."

"She wished for a bridge." Mallory calmed herself. "I mean, a kiss on a bridge. From a hero."

"As in, Superman?"

If anyone asked, I'd say yes. "Buzz does have an air of *super-ness* about him."

Beatrix nodded. "And, is he your hero?"

Oh, yes. The best! I told her a little of Buzz's background. Not too much, just enough. "But the wish did pan out."

"Yeah, but Emily had to buy her own bridge to make it work." Mallory patted my arm. "Good thinking, by the way."

"And you," I aimed my comments at Mallory, "needed to peel back the layers and find the royalty beneath sawdust-covered flannel shirts." I turned to Jayne. "And you needed to see what was right in front of your eyes."

"He was there all along. It just took a perfectly horrible perfect Christmas at a snowy lodge to see it."

Beatrix hugged her knees and rested her chin on them. "If it worked for you, will it work for me?" Her voice held longing. Wistfulness. I got that—I'd felt that way just last year, when my every step had been plagued by the chant *I'm the last one left. I'm the last one left.*

"Yes!" Mallory cried. "You're wonderful, Beatrix, so you of all people deserve it. The second you see a snowfall, grab that first snowflake, okay? Make that wish!"

I patted Beatrix's knee. "It does help if you're pretty specific, and you can't just wait around. You have to put yourself somewhere it can happen."

"Do you know what you wish already?" Jayne, donning her reporter persona, asked. "Or is it something you'd rather not share?"

Beatrix patted her camera. "I think I'd better get back to the reason I'm here." She stood and asked us three to lean our heads together. "Say, *true love.*"

We said it, smiling, and Beatrix snapped the picture.

"Beatrix," Mallory said, "come be in the picture. We'll find someone to snap it."

"Me?" Beatrix waved her off. "Not me. I'm more of a behind the camera person, not someone in front of it."

Buzz poked his head into the white silk tent, its fabric billowing. "You all ready for the rehearsal dinner?" He came over and took my hands. "I love that you chose the menu of waffles with maple syrup."

"Everyone secretly loves breakfast for dinner. And Maplebrook Farm has the most perfect syrup in the world."

"You mean the most perfect sap in the world." He kissed me until Jayne and Mallory clapped for us. That kiss blurred into the next after the rehearsal dinner, and our goodnight kiss of the night-before-our-wedding, and finally into the kiss when the preacher standing on the beautiful back lawn of Seacliff Chateau pronounced us husband and wife.

To say that wishes come true seems trite. It sounds so impossible, so naïve. But I knew better now. Because Buzz had come into my life in such a convoluted but miraculous way. And Buzz was my every wish come true.

Snowfall Wishes Series

Wildwood Lodge

Seacliff Chateau

Maplebrook Bridge

Palisades Point

Acknowledgments

Thanks go to the wonderful staff at the Eastern Arizona College Library for their incredible support and accommodation while this book was created.

Many thanks to Donna Hatch, Mary Mintz, and Paula Bothwell, without whose help this book wouldn't have come into being.

More thanks to Suzy, Dacia, Debbie, and Jeanie for giving early encouragement.

Also, huge gratitude to Shaela at Blue Water Books for her gorgeous covers. You have a wonderful talent and a beautiful soul.

Finally, never-ending thanks to my husband, who is my "alpha reader" and first in everything in my heart.

About the Author

Jennifer Griffith is the *USA Today* bestselling author of clean, escapist fiction she calls Cotton Candy for the Soul. She and her family live in the rural Arizona desert, where the winter is seldom snowy, but she loves Christmas and cocoa and all things cozy.

Made in the USA
Columbia, SC
04 February 2022